Praise for Kate Hoffmann's Mighty Quinns

"This truly delightful tale packs in the heat
and a lot of heart at the same time."
—*RT Book Reviews* on *The Mighty Quinns: Dermot*

"This is a fast read that is hard to tear the eyes from.
Once I picked it up I couldn't put it down."
—*Fresh Fiction* on *The Mighty Quinns: Dermot*

"A story that not only pulled me in,
but left me weak in the knees."
—*Seriously Reviewed* on *The Mighty Quinns: Riley*

"Sexy, heartwarming and romantic, this is a story to
settle down with and enjoy—and then reread."
—*RT Book Reviews* on *The Mighty Quinns: Teague*

"Sexy Irish folklore and intrigue
weave throughout this steamy tale."
—*RT Book Reviews* on *The Mighty Quinns: Kellan*

"The only drawback to this story
is that it's far too short!"
—*Fresh Fiction* on *The Mighty Quinns: Kellan*

"Strong, imperfect but lovable characters,
an interesting setting and great sensuality."
—*RT Book Reviews* on *The Mighty Quinns: Brody*

Dear Reader,

It's hard to believe that I've been writing for Harlequin for nearly twenty years. It seems like only yesterday that I completed my first novel and sent it in, hoping that it would be good enough to publish. Now, many books later, people sometimes ask if I ever run out of ideas. Fortunately, I don't. There always seems to be a line of characters just waiting to have their story written.

This month I kick off another set of Mighty Quinns. Only, this time I'm doing something a little different— I'm setting the stories in four different countries! This first book, *The Mighty Quinns: Logan,* takes place in Australia, and the next book, *The Mighty Quinns: Jack,* will bring you back to the U.S. The last two books are still in progress, so I won't give out any spoilers just yet. But you might want to watch out for a couple of hot Irish guys named Rourke and Dex.... :)

As always, without you I wouldn't have the chance to continue to tell my stories. Whether you've been with me from the start or you've just discovered my books, thank you for reading! Be sure to check out my page on Facebook for all the latest news.

All my best,

Kate Hoffmann

The Mighty Quinns: Logan

—

Kate Hoffmann

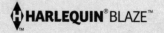

Recycling programs
for this product may
not exist in your area.

ISBN-13: 978-0-373-79739-4

THE MIGHTY QUINNS: LOGAN

HARLEQUIN®
™ www.Harlequin.com

Printed in U.S.A.

ABOUT THE AUTHOR

Kate Hoffmann has written more than seventy books for Harlequin, most of them for the Temptation and Blaze lines. She spent time as a music teacher, a retail assistant buyer and an advertising exec before she settled into a career as a full-time writer. She continues to pursue her interests in music, theater and musical theater, working with local schools in various productions. She lives in southeastern Wisconsin with her cat, Chloe.

Books by Kate Hoffmann

HARLEQUIN BLAZE

HARLEQUIN SINGLE TITLES

For Michelle. Never stop believing.
It can happen for you, too!

Prologue

DROPLETS OF RAIN spattered against the wavy glass in the manor-house windows. Aileen Quinn stared out into the lush green of her garden, her gaze fixed on a niche in the tall stone wall. A small statue of an angel was nestled into the ivy, the rain dripping off the outspread wings as if it wept.

"Are you certain?" she asked.

"I know this is a lot to handle, Miss Quinn. Perhaps we should continue later?"

She gripped the head of her cane and turned back to the genealogist. "No," she said. "I'm ninety-six years old. There will be no more secrets in my life. That's why I chose to write my autobiography. I want it all out there so I can leave this world in peace."

"You realize the chances that your older siblings are still alive are virtually zero."

Aileen moved to a wing chair near the fireplace and sat down, turning toward the warmth. "Of course. But I would like to know if they had children and grandchildren. I have a family and I'd like to know at least a little bit about them before I die."

She stared into the flickering flames, her thoughts carrying her back to her childhood. She only had the thinnest of details, facts that the nuns at the orphanage had relinquished after years of persistent questions. Her father had died in the Easter Rising of 1916, shot through the heart by a British soldier. Her mother, left pregnant and desperate to provide for her newborn daughter, grew sick with consumption and brought Aileen to the orphanage a few weeks before she died.

The story had been told so many times in the media, the rags-to-riches tale of an Irish orphan girl who became one of the world's most popular novelists. Aileen's stories had been a reflection of her life, tales of struggle and triumph, of heartache and great happiness, and all set in the land of her birth, her beautiful Ireland.

"Tell me again," she said. "Their names. What were my brothers' names?"

"The eldest was Diarmuid. He was twelve when he was sent off to work as an apprentice to a shipbuilder in Belfast in 1917. Then there was Conal. He was nine and Lochlan was six when you were born. And Tomas was five. There were three other children who didn't survive. A baby girl between Diarmuid and Conal who died at birth. And a daughter named Mary and a son named Orin between Tomas and you. They both died of scarlet fever the year before you were born."

"So there were seven, not four."

The young man nodded. "Yes."

"I need to know where they went," Aileen said, leaning forward in her chair. "How they lived. You need to find everything you can about them."

"Yes, ma'am," he said. He riffled through his papers. "I was able to learn that the youngest, Tomas, was sent to Australia. He traveled with a missionary and his wife on a ship called the *Cambria,* which sailed from Cork and landed in Sydney in December of 1916."

"Then that's where you'll begin," Aileen said. "In Australia. I don't care how many people you need to hire to help you or how much it costs. I'm giving you unlimited funds to do whatever is needed, Mr. Stephens. And I want a weekly report of any progress you've made, no matter how inconsequential."

"Yes, Miss Quinn."

"That's all for now," she said.

He nodded and walked out of the solarium, his research tucked under his arm. Aileen watched him leave, then drew a deep breath. She'd spent her whole life believing she was alone in the world, a victim of circumstances beyond her control. But now, in a single instant, she had a family, siblings who had once held her and kissed her…and loved her.

The housekeeper walked into the room, her footsteps silent on the ornate rug. Sally set the tray down on the tea table. "I've baked some lovely scones," she said. "Will you not have one?"

Aileen shook her head. "Just the tea, Sally."

"Did your Mr. Stephens have anything interesting to share?"

"Not at the present," she replied. The news about her family was so startling that she wanted to keep it a secret just a bit longer. It wasn't a good thing to hope. She'd learned that as a child, every Sunday, when visiting day at Our Lady of Mercy orphanage arrived. Just over a hundred girls, dressed in their very best, would stand in proper rows, hoping that someone would come, would choose to take one of them home.

But she'd been a sickly child, smaller than the others and plagued with respiratory infections, and often pushed into the background. After a time, she'd decided to stop trying. She was safe with the nuns and had dreams of joining the Sisters of St. Clare herself.

The orphanage provided a harsh type of life. Punishments were meted out regularly for the girls who refused to conform. Those that were considered chronically impure—the illegitimate, the criminal, the intractable—bore the brunt of the nuns' disdain. But Aileen was pious and penitent for even the slightest sin.

When Sister Mary gave her a coveted job in the

school library, shelving books and reading to the younger girls, she'd quietly been marked as a favorite and was spared the worst of chores.

By the time she was eleven, she'd run out of books to read in the school library and was allowed to accompany the lively young teacher, Sister Bernadette, to the Kinsale library, where she'd been handed a copy of *Jane Eyre* and told to hide it from the older nuns.

The book had opened a whole new world for her. The story of the plain orphan girl, snatched from her cruel fate and whisked into a life as a governess, had been a revelation. How was it possible to put words in such an order that they could create a truth in her mind?

From that moment on, Aileen had begun to write her own stories, at first just weak copies of what she read. But as her methodical march through the town library shelves continued, she learned more about how to craft a plot and develop a character.

In the evenings, she'd offered to empty the rubbish bins at school, just for the chance to gather spare paper for her work. And then, when she was in the seventh form, Sister Bernadette became her teacher. The sweet-tempered nun recognized Aileen's talent for writing. From that moment on, Aileen always had pencils and tablets to spare, and someone to read her stories.

Though the girls at the orphanage were trained

toward industrial employment, Aileen had been encouraged in her plans to devote her life to God and join the order as a novitiate. But the closer she got to the decision, the more Aileen knew that the life she wanted, and the stories swimming around in her head, couldn't be contained within the walls of the convent. She'd have to go out in the world and make her own way, to live the life that she so desperately wanted to write about.

And so she did what Jane Eyre had done. She became a governess for a wealthy family in Dublin, moving from the orphanage into a grand home situated on a posh street. She cared for three boys by the name of Riley while their father ran a bank and their mother busied herself with charitable works.

And at night, after the boys had been tucked into bed, she wrote. And wrote and wrote and wrote. She saved her meager salary and bought a secondhand typewriter for her twenty-first birthday, then spent what she had left on paper and inked ribbon.

At night, she'd sneak up to a far corner of the attic, lantern in hand, so that the family wouldn't hear the tap-tap-tap of the keys. She sold her first novel five years later, the story of an orphaned Irish girl who falls in love with the son of her employer, only to be cast aside and left to rebuild a life for herself. Set between the two world wars, the novel sold well enough for her to leave the Rileys and rent a tiny flat in a run-down section of Dublin.

Now, seventy years later, Aileen Quinn had become the grande dame of Irish women writers, the one they all referenced when they talked of their greatest influences. She'd won every award and accolade available to her and had enjoyed her life and her success.

Her only regret had been that the love her characters always struggled to find had never found her. She'd always thought there would be time for a husband and a family. But the years between thirty and fifty had seemed to fly by in a blur. Then, she'd still hoped a man might come into her life. And then another blur between fifty and seventy. By then it was too late for hope. Too late to have a family of her own.

But all that had changed now. She did have a family, people who were related to her by blood. And she was going to find every last one of them.

1

LOGAN QUINN STARED down the long, tree-lined driveway. He'd expected Willimston Farm would be upmarket, but he hadn't expected a feckin' estate. He turned the campervan off the main road and felt a sense of unease come over him.

When he'd made plans to stop along his weeklong route to Perth, all Logan had wanted was a spare stable, fresh water and a place to park. His old mate Ed Perkins had been working as a stable manager at Willimston for the past few years and had offered a place to overnight. Logan wondered how Ed's boss man might feel about the raggedy campervan and trailer ruining the perfectly groomed landscape.

If the sprawling house didn't give visitors a clue to the wealth of the owners, the outbuildings did. The low-slung buildings were painted white with green doors and shingles, a clear indication of the bottomless bank account that funded the place. Logan couldn't help but think of his own ranch on the fringes of the outback, the ramshackle house, the rough stables.

He'd worked for years to put together the cash needed to buy his own operation, sometimes juggling his job as an investment banker with one or two other jobs. And though the ranch was far from perfect, it was the first home he'd ever known.

After a childhood spent watching his father bounce from place to place, sheep station to cattle ranch, all the family's belongings contained in the back of a pickup truck, Logan needed a place to put down roots.

Every time he drove up the dusty road and saw the weathered stable and tiny house, he felt a measure of pride. He was building something for the future. And maybe someday, he'd have a family and they'd know a real home, a place where they could feel safe and secure.

A kid couldn't help but feel that way on Willimston Farm, he thought to himself. "Someday, my place will look like this," he murmured. Logan chuckled to himself. "Yeah, right. And someday, pigs will fly."

He slowly pulled the campervan to a stop and turned off the ignition. They'd been on the road for eight hours. It was time for the both of them to stretch their legs. He watched as a tall, lanky figure approached, then recognized his old friend Ed beneath the brim of the faded hat.

Logan stepped out of the camper and pulled off his sunglasses. "Ed! Hey, mate. Good to see you."

Ed yanked off his leather gloves and shook Logan's hand. "Logan Quinn. How was your drive?"

"Long. It feels good to stand instead of sit." He glanced around. "This is quite the place. You landed yourself a nice spot."

"It's good. The owner isn't around much. He has a mansion in Brisbane, too. But when he is here, he's a decent chap. Simon Grant. He's big in energy. Appreciates fine horses, too. So, who's watching your place while you're on the road?"

"I've got Billy Brantley working for me. Remember him? He worked with us that summer out on the Weaver ranch."

"He's a good guy. Hard worker." Ed nodded in the direction of the trailer. "Enough of this chatter. Are you going to show me?"

"Sure. Let's get her out." Logan walked to the back of the trailer, dropped the ramp and opened the doors. He smoothed his hand over the flank of the filly as he moved to take her halter.

"Come on, darlin'," he murmured. "Let's get you out of this trailer and into a paddock. You need some exercise." The filly slowly backed down the ramp and, when all four hooves were on firm ground,

Logan circled her around Ed, letting him observe the horse.

He'd never been more proud of something that he'd accomplished as he had been of breeding and raising Tally. And though he knew not to get too attached to one of his horses, Logan was forced to admit that he loved everything about the pretty filly.

"Jaysus, Logan, she's a beauty." Ed stepped forward and examined the filly with a keen eye. He ran his palms over her, peered into her eyes and patted her neck. "You say she's sold?"

"Why? Do you want to buy her?"

"Hell, I'd be crazy not to show her to my boss. He's always looking for new stock."

Logan shrugged. "Yeah, she's sold. To a guy over in Perth. He's got a nice breeding operation."

"No. How much?"

Logan told him the price and Ed shrugged. "It's a fair price. I probably could have gotten you more. I would have liked to breed her with a stallion we have. They would have made some beautiful babies together." He paused. "Why didn't you keep her for yourself?"

A sliver of regret shot through him at the question. "I would have loved to. But I need the money."

"Things are tough?"

Logan chuckled. "Define *tough*."

"Why didn't you give me a call? I could have helped you out."

"You're helping me out now. Letting me stay here for the night. Now, do you have a paddock for my lady? I think she could use a good run."

"Come on, then. I saved the best for you."

They walked toward one of the low barns and when they reached the paddock, Ed opened the gate. Logan rubbed the filly's neck then sent her inside. She trotted around the perimeter, her ears up, her nostrils sniffing the air.

"What's her name?"

"I call her Tally," he said. "Her official name is Quinn's Tally-Ho Wallaroo. But maybe the new owners will give her a different name."

"She is a beauty."

Logan nodded. "Yeah. She's the first colt born on the farm, the first I raised from a baby. Hell, I feel like she's my kid and I'm sending her off into the world."

Ed patted him on the shoulder. "I expect letting the first one go is always the hardest. I've set up a stall in this barn here," he said, pointing over his shoulder. "You can pull your campervan around to the back. Just inside the door there's a loo and a shower."

"Thanks," he said.

"Have you had dinner yet?"

"Yeah. I picked up something along the way. Once I have Tally bedded down, I'm going to turn in, too. I'm knackered."

"Well, I'm up at sunrise. I'll bring you some breakfast before you leave."

Logan nodded. "Thanks. For everything. I really appreciate it."

"No worries," Ed said.

As Ed walked back to the stable, Logan turned his gaze out to the chestnut filly in the paddock. He'd always thought that Tally would be the center of his breeding program at the farm. He'd never imagined that he'd have to give her up. Just the thought of turning her over into someone else's care caused an ache deep in his gut. But horse breeding was like roulette. Sometimes you hit the jackpot and other times you walked away with nothing.

He braced his arms on the top of the gate and rested his chin on his hands. He'd had a choice. Keep the horse or keep the ranch. Without the filly, the ranch would survive. Without the ranch, he had no place to keep his horses.

Hell, maybe another filly like Tally would come along. Though her sire and dam had produced two males in the past two years, the odds were good that he was due a filly. But what were the chances that she'd be as perfect as Tally? He'd hate to think that his one-in-a-million horse had come at a time when he couldn't keep her for himself.

A quiet curse slipped from his lips. This trip wouldn't be any easier if he continued to drown in sentimentality.

"Nice horse."

The sound of her voice startled him. Logan turned to find a woman standing beside him on the lowest rail of the gate. The sun was behind her and he had a hard time making out her features, so he stepped back from the gate and pulled down his sunglasses.

The beauty of her profile, outlined by the setting sun, hit him like a ton of bricks. Flaxen hair gleamed in the golden light, the strands falling around her face in delicate curls. She looked as if she'd just crawled out of bed.

Her eyes were hidden behind dark sunglasses. She wore a loose-fitting T-shirt and the bottoms to a hot-pink bikini that barely covered her backside. The soft curves of her breasts were outlined by the thin cotton, and he could almost imagine the body beneath the shirt. His gaze drifted back up to her face and he took in her lush lips.

A tiny smile twitched at the corners of that sensuous mouth. "What's next? Are you going to want to check my teeth? Maybe run your hands over my withers? I can take a turn around the paddock if you like."

He hadn't realized his stare was so obvious. He turned away and fixed his gaze on Tally. "You—you startled me."

"Good," she said. "I always like making a memorable first impression."

He laughed softly. She was teasing him and wasn't

trying to hide it. But to what end? "Well done, then," he said. "I'm impressed." Logan glanced over at her. "Who are you?"

She held out her hand. "Lucinda Grant. My father owns this place."

He took her hand and gave it a quick shake. Her fingers were long and slender and tipped with shiny red polish. His mind flashed an image of those hands, skimming over his naked body, touching him in places he hadn't been touched for a while. Logan swallowed hard. Yeah, right. No chance a pretty little rich girl was going to waste her time on guy without a penny in his pocket.

"Nice to meet you, Miss Grant," Logan said.

"Oh, please. You stared at my arse. I think we're beyond Miss Grant. You can call me Sunny."

"I thought your name was Lucinda."

"It is, but everyone calls me Sunny. With a *u*. Actually, it really should be an *o*. My father always wanted a boy so he called me Sonny with an *o* until I was five. My mother changed it to Sunny with a *u*."

"It's nice to meet you, Sunny with a *u*."

She pushed her sunglasses onto the top of her head and turned her green-eyed gaze his way. "It's usually customary for you to tell me your name. You really do have the worst manners."

"Are you always such a smart-ass?" he asked, starting to enjoy the little game they were playing.

That brought a laugh. "I developed the talent in

my teenage years and have perfected it since then. It's one of my best qualities."

He saw the glint in her gaze and Logan shook his head. He'd known girls like her, girls who weren't afraid to push the boundaries, girls who would say anything that came into their heads just to get a re-action. He usually made it a point to stay away from that type. They were impossible to figure out.

But there was something about Sunny, something more than just a quick wit and a sharp tongue. He saw something more…vulnerable behind that bold facade. He could see it in those eyes, those incred-ibly beautiful green eyes.

Logan rubbed his hand on his faded jeans before holding it out to her. "Logan Quinn."

She stared down at his hand for a long moment and Logan wondered if she didn't want to touch him. But then, she reached out and ran her finger along the length of his forearm. The feel of her nail scraping his skin sent a shiver through his body. She glanced up at him and smiled coyly. "You have nice hands, Logan Quinn." Her gaze turned toward the filly, who was now watching them both with a suspicious eye. "Is she yours?"

"For now," Logan said.

With that, she crawled over the gate and dropped down on the other side, her bare feet causing a soft thud in the dirt. As she walked toward Tally, Sunny turned back to him. "Come on," she said. "I want to hear what you have to say about her."

Logan followed her over the gate and hurried to catch up. As he walked beside her, he risked a glance at her face again. God, she was the prettiest thing he'd ever seen. And the oddest, as well. She didn't seem to be bothered by the fact that she was wandering around in a T-shirt that was just thin enough to reveal what was underneath. Maybe she'd spent the day sunbathing...topless.... He swallowed hard as a vivid image flashed in his mind.

When they got within ten feet of the filly, Sunny stopped and held out her hand. "What's her name?"

"Tally," he said.

"Hey, there, Tally," she murmured.

Logan reached in his jacket pocket and pulled out a biscuit, then handed it to her. "She likes these."

"Anzac biscuits? Me, too." She took a bite from the biscuit, then held the treat out to Tally. The horse immediately walked over and snatched the biscuit from Sunny's fingers.

Gently, she grabbed her halter and led the horse in a wide circle. Logan watched Sunny, his attention completely captivated by her long, slender legs and her lithe body. He felt a current of desire skitter through him and he drew a long breath.

Sunny carefully examined the horse, smoothing her palms over Tally, slowly taking in her conformation. And when she was finished, she motioned him over.

"Give me a knee up," she said.

"You're going to ride her?"

"Why not?"

Logan linked his fingers together and she slipped her knee into the cradle. He boosted her up and Sunny gracefully straddled the horse. Tangling her fingers in Tally's mane, she gave the filly a gentle nudge, and Tally moved forward.

The sight of them both, a beautiful woman and an equally beautiful horse, was enough to take Logan's breath away. His pulse quickened and he found himself searching for his next breath. As she urged Tally into a gallop, he groaned, trying to keep his mind off the images running around in his head.

It had been months since he'd enjoyed the company of a woman in his bed. Hell, in any bed. Life on the ranch was filled with plenty of time for self-reflection. When it came to women, he didn't have much of anything to offer besides a really good time in the sack. After buying feed for his horses, he usually didn't have much left for himself, so even a dinner out or a movie would be out of the question. But the sale of Tally would keep him solvent for another year and perhaps available for dating.

He fixed his attention on Sunny. There was no way a woman like her would want a bloke like him. No way. But that wouldn't stop him from using her as fantasy material. His fingers clenched as he thought about touching her—her hair, her face, her beautiful body.

Sunny brought the horse to a stop in front of him and slid off. "Whatever Daddy offers you, ask for 50 percent more. And don't back down. He admires a man who sticks to his principles." She started toward the gate. "I'll see you later, Logan Quinn."

"Wait!" he called. He took off after her and caught up with Sunny after she'd crawled over the gate. "She's not for sale. Tally isn't for sale—at least, not to you—or your father."

Sunny gave him an odd look, her forehead furrowed. "Then what are you doing here?"

He drew a deep breath. "Just…passing through."

Silence spun out around them, and his gaze drifted to her lips. He wanted to kiss her, just once, just to see how her mouth felt on his, how she tasted and how she reacted. It took every ounce of his will-power to stop himself from pulling her into his arms. But the gate stood between them, as great a barrier as anything else that separated them.

She sucked in a sharp breath and, suddenly, the silence was broken, along with the spell that had overcome them both. "She's still a beautiful horse," Sunny murmured.

Logan watched her walk away, her hips swaying provocatively. He'd never met a woman quite like her. So tantalizing, so sexy. "Forget it, mate," he muttered to himself. "That's the first and last time a woman like that is ever giving you a second look."

SUNNY STARED UP at the ceiling above her bed. She measured her breathing, trying to fight back the surge of tears that had been threatening for the past hour. Grabbing her pillow, she hugged it to her body, but nothing seemed to ease the emptiness inside of her.

Her thoughts wandered back to the argument she'd had with her father earlier that evening. He'd phoned from Sydney to check up on her plans to participate in an equestrian event that weekend in Brisbane. When she told him she had no intention of riding, the call escalated into a cold recitation of all of her flaws as both a daughter and a human being.

She pinched her eyes shut, cutting off the source of her tears. Nighttime was the worst. Her mind just wouldn't shut down. The same things replayed over and over in her head, and though she tried to make sense of it all, she couldn't.

She'd worked for years to get to London, to be a part of the Olympics and to show her father that she could be just as good as the son he'd always wanted. All the training, all the travel, competing in equestrian events all over Australia.

Three years ago, she'd stepped up to international competition, all with an eye to the Olympics and her crowning achievement, a gold medal in show jumping. When she made the world team two years ago, her father had been delighted but reserved. When she made the Olympic team, her father had been proud, ecstatic even. And that's all she'd ever wanted from him. Just a simple recognition that she was someone worth loving.

But what had come next had been so unexpected. She'd landed in London with a strange sense of foreboding, a dark cloud hanging over her. The pressure to succeed just seemed overwhelming at times and she found herself fighting off panic attacks.

One stumble in the qualifying rounds had led to another and by the time the preliminary competition was over, Sunny's confidence was in shreds and her hopes for a medal were gone. She had hesitated when she should have been aggressive; she had tried to make up for her mistakes by taking silly risks. And her sweet horse, Padma, didn't understand what she was supposed to do, the unfamiliar signals causing the mare to react nervously and refuse gates that she'd always nimbly jumped over.

A tear streaked down Sunny's cheek and she brushed it away. Who was she if she wasn't an equestrian? Where was she supposed to go from here? She wasn't prepared to do anything but ride. Her life was a total car wreck with no one there to help her fix it.

With a long sigh, she closed her eyes. The image of Logan Quinn drifted through her thoughts and she groaned softly. She'd been thinking about him all night long. If he knew who she was, he didn't mention it. And if he didn't, then he must have been living on another continent for the past six months. The media had been brutal right after the games, with all sorts of rumors about partying and drugs and men.

None of it had been true, but that didn't make it any less painful. She smiled to herself. It had felt good to talk to Logan, to tease and laugh again, as if nothing had happened. Part of the attraction was his body, lean and muscled, hidden beneath faded, comfortable clothes. And he had that rugged, self-assured look about him, as though he could survive for a month in the outback with just a paper clip and a piece of string. He had a quiet confidence that was reassuring.

For the first time in months, Sunny found herself interested in something other than her own troubles. And though seducing a handsome stranger probably wouldn't change her situation all that much, it would be nice to feel close to someone. It would give her something else to think about at night other than all her failures.

Sunny rolled onto her stomach and pressed her face into the pillow. What if he wasn't interested? What if he didn't want anything to do with her? Leave it to Sunny Grant to fail on both a worldwide and a personal scale.

Sunny sat up in bed and tossed the pillow aside. She had to stop doing this to herself. It was time to

move on. She'd made mistakes and hadn't been prepared to handle the pressure, but there was no going
back and fixing it. If she ever expected to be happy
again, she needed to—

"I need to get out of this house," she muttered,
raking her hair away from her face.

Scrambling out of bed, Sunny grabbed a robe and
shrugged into it. Silently, she slipped out of her room
and hurried down the hall. The house was dark and
only the dogs, Wendy and Whip, noticed her passing, their heads rising as she opened the kitchen door.

She drew a deep breath of the warm night air,
then ran across the damp lawn to the stables. A yel-
low bulb on each end of the building offered a faint
light and she hurried to Padma's stall and pulled
open the door.

The horse turned and looked at her with her big
brown eyes. Sunny hadn't ridden her in the three
months since she'd returned from London, knowing
how she'd failed. "I'm sorry," she murmured, tears
filling her eyes. "I'm so sorry. You're the only one
who has ever loved me, unconditionally and without any expectations. And I let you down. I embarrassed us both."

Her father had talked about selling Padma after
Sunny had vowed never to ride again. The horse
was well trained, an experienced competitor in the
prime of her jumping career. But she was still here,

in her usual stable. Though her father could be cold, he wasn't entirely heartless.

"You're going to be just fine," she murmured, stroking the white blaze on Padma's forehead. "I need to take a little more time away and then I'll be back and we'll start all over again. I promise. We'll get back to the top and get our gold medal." She pressed her face against the soft muzzle of the horse, then gave her a kiss. "And this time, I won't mess it up. You'll be proud of me."

She stepped out of the stall and pulled the door closed. When she turned, she saw a figure standing in the shadows. A gasp slipped from her throat, but when he stepped into the light, she recognized Logan Quinn.

"You scared me," she said.

"Sorry. I didn't mean to. I was just checking on Tally and heard you talking."

He was dressed in just his jeans, the top button undone. Like her, his feet were bare. He'd shoved his hands in his front pockets and he watched her warily. "It's late," she murmured.

"I couldn't sleep. It was too stuffy in the campervan."

"Me, too," she said.

"It is kind of warm tonight. I thought maybe we'd get some rain."

She smiled to herself. He looked so sweet standing there, his dark hair rumpled, his chest bare. Though he looked as if he were in his late twenties, he had a boyish quality she found undeniably attractive. "Are we really talking about the weather?"

"No," he said.

Sunny held out her hand. "Come with me."

He tucked his hand into hers and walked with her toward the house. "Where are we going?"

"You'll see," she said.

There was a formal garden in the rear of the house, surrounded by a tall iron fence. She unlatched the gate and then stepped aside, motioning for him to enter. They walked along a narrow brick path and, suddenly, the lush greenery disappeared and he found himself staring at a huge swimming pool.

"Oh, hell. Now, that's a nice-looking pool."

"Come on. Take your jeans off and jump in."

"Ah, I don't have anything underneath," he said.

She reached for the tie of her silk robe. "You don't have anything I haven't seen before." Sunny spun around in front of him. "And I don't have anything you haven't seen before."

With a laugh, she dove into the pool, slicing neatly into the water and swimming beneath the surface to the other end. When she came up for air, he was no longer standing on the deck. She glanced around and then, a moment later, he popped up in front of her.

"What are your parents going to say if they catch us out here?" he asked.

"My father is in Sydney, visiting his mistress

and their two children. My mother went to the Paris fashion shows last year and never came back." She reached out and brushed the wet hair out of his eyes. "Except for the housekeeper, we're alone."

"Okay, then."

"You don't talk very much, do you?"

He grinned. "Actually, I do. You just leave me a little speechless."

She bobbed in front of him, her gaze taking in the details of his face. Droplets clung to his dark lashes, and when he blinked, they tumbled onto his cheeks. He was a beautiful man, the kind of man who didn't realize the effect his looks had on a woman. She liked that. Sunny didn't know very many regular guys.

His body was finely muscled, long limbed and lean, and made that way by hard work. The attraction was undeniable, but could she act on it? She'd felt so alone for such a long time, trapped in a life that had no direction or purpose. Touching him, kissing him, was all she could think about.

And what harm could it do? She'd enjoyed one-night stands in the past. The man was leaving in the morning and she'd never see him again. Why not take advantage? The thought of losing herself for just a short time with this beautiful man was more than she could resist.

Sunny placed her hands on his shoulders, her gaze fixed on his lips. She leaned forward ever so slightly and he took the cue, slipping his fingers through the wet hair at her nape and pulling her into his kiss. A wave of desire coursed through her body, and the intensity of her reaction startled her.

He knew how to kiss, that much was clear. And Sunny had kissed enough men to make a valid comparison. He began softly, his lips teasing at hers until they were both ready to taste. And then, he used his tongue to test her further, to tempt her into surrender. She parted her lips and they were suddenly lost in a whirlwind of sensation.

Had there ever been a kiss that affected her so completely? She felt her limbs go weak and her mind begin to falter. When his hands moved to her face, she moaned softly and wrapped her arms around his neck. Logan reached down for her legs, pulling them around his waist until their bodies were locked together in an unbreakable embrace.

He was already hard, and she moved against him, resisting the urge to simply sink down on top of him. She knew they ought to find a condom before they went any further, but if she brought up the realities of protection, he might have a chance to reconsider what they were about to do.

Drawing a deep breath, she unlocked her legs and pushed away, swimming to the far end of the pool. "I could get in a lot of trouble with a boy like you," she said, sinking down until her chin touched the surface.

She'd always maintained control in her casual encounters. There was never anything beyond the physical satisfaction of being with a beautiful man. But she felt something different with Logan, something that made her want him even more. It was as if they already knew each other, and yet she knew nothing about him.

Sunny brushed the water out of her face. She wanted to be with him, to experience the sensation of his body moving inside of her. "Do you want me?" she asked softly.

Logan nodded. "I'd be a fool not to."

"It's only about the sex," she said. "Nothing else. Are you all right with that?"

He nodded again as he slowly approached. "Here?"

She shook her head. "We need protection."

"I have some in the campervan."

Sunny swam over to the ladder and then slowly climbed it to the pool deck. She grabbed a towel from a nearby bin and wrapped it around her body, then handed one to Logan. He hurried after her, and when he reached her side, he took her hand. They walked back to the stable, Logan picking up his jeans and her robe along the way.

A cool breeze rustled the trees, and goose pimples prickled Sunny's damp skin. For the first time since London, she knew exactly what she wanted. And there was no shame in it. The need to feel close to another person was a basic part of human nature, wasn't it? And since Logan was just passing through, it made the choice even easier. There would be no messy entanglements after the fact.

Raindrops were beginning to fall by the time they reached the campervan. Logan opened the door and helped her up the steps. All the windows were open, and the sound of the rain on the roof provided a relaxing soundtrack. A tiny light near the sink provided the only illumination, casting the interior in a soft glow.

When he closed the door behind him, Sunny turned and stepped into his embrace. There was no hesitation between them, no doubt of what they both wanted, no time wasted. The towels were tossed aside, and his hands moved over her body, his touch gentle yet assured. Sunny closed her eyes and tipped her head back, letting the wonderful sensations wash over her.

When his lips finally found hers, Sunny opened to the determined assault. He was warm and his mouth tasted sweet and when he pulled her body against his, she surrendered completely. It had been months since she'd felt any kind of connection to a man. But now that he had dropped into her life, Sunny felt desperate to experience the power and the passion, the complete and utter satisfaction.

Though there was no reason to rush, Sunny had never been one to deny herself anything she wanted.

And she wanted to experience the ultimate intimacy with this man. She pulled him over to the bed that spanned the back end of the campervan.

Logan sat down on the edge and smoothed his hands around her waist. "Are you certain about this?" he murmured, pressing a kiss to her belly.

Sunny ran her fingers through his sun-streaked hair and turned his face up until his gaze met hers. "I wouldn't be here if I didn't know what I wanted," she murmured.

He smiled and she reached down and ran her thumb across his lower lip. He was so beautiful, his hair damp from their swim, his skin smooth and deeply tanned. Falling back onto the bed, he reached into a nearby cubby and pulled out a box of condoms, setting them beside a pillow.

Sunny held out her hand, wiggling her fingers, and he pulled a package from the box and handed it to her. He held his breath as she slowly stroked his hard shaft. A low groan slipped from his throat, and he leaned back and braced himself on his elbows, his gaze fixed on her caress.

With a deft touch, she smoothed the latex over him, then crawled onto the bed, her legs straddling his hips. She couldn't wait any longer, she craved that exquisite sensation of a man moving inside her.

Sunny closed her eyes as she slowly lowered herself on top of him. When he filled her completely, she let out a soft breath. There was nothing more perfect than this, she thought to herself. As his fingers splayed over her hips, she began to move. When Logan cupped her face in his hand, she turned into his touch and looked at him.

Their gazes locked, and Sunny watched as every reaction was reflected in his eyes. A smile curled the corners of his mouth, and she felt a tremor course through her, setting every nerve on edge. There was something about him, something sweet and warm and slightly vulnerable, that made it impossible to separate herself from the emotion bubbling up inside of her.

Another tremor assailed her body, but this time it wasn't pleasure but fear. This connection wasn't normal. She'd always been able to maintain a careful distance with the men she took as lovers. But for the first time in her life, she wanted to surrender everything, to let the walls fall and experience this man as if there were something more than just desire between them.

Logan pushed up from the bed and wrapped his arms around her waist, pressing his lips to a spot just above her breast. Sunny could feel her heart pounding, and the sudden shift in position bought a fresh rush of desire.

She pulled him closer, her fingers tangled in his hair. The rhythm became like a pulse between them, driving them on, pushing them both closer and closer to the edge. It was nothing she'd ever experienced before, and she fought the instinct to stop and regain her composure.

Sunny didn't realize it until she was teetering on the brink between pleasure and release. It usually didn't happen this way, but when the first spasm hit her, she cried out. Logan held her close as he drove into her one last time. And then they both dissolved into their climaxes, the shudders and sighs blending until she felt as if they were one body and one mind.

When they were both completely spent, Logan pulled her down beside him, wrapping his arms around her shoulders. They didn't speak, just looked into each other's eyes for a long time. There was something about this man that was different, something about him that touched her soul.

"I should go," she murmured.

"You don't have to. Stay. I'm not tired."

She always left, she never stayed. And yet, the rules she'd set down for herself so long ago didn't really matter now. It felt good to lie here with this man and to share something beyond the physical.

"Are you really going to sell your horse?"

Logan nodded. "Yeah. I'm taking her to Perth."

"That's a long drive. At least a week on the road. Why not put her on a plane?"

Logan was silent for a long time. "I guess I needed the time to get used to the fact I have to sell her. Plus, I'm saving some money."

"Maybe you should stay here for a few days and

let me try to change your mind," she said. "I'd take good care of her."

He chuckled softly. "That's an interesting proposition."

"Is it one you'd consider?"

Logan reached out and smoothed a strand of hair from her eyes. "I can't. I'm kind of pressed for time. And I've already spent the down payment. The sooner I get this over with, the better."

"I can give you the down payment," she said. "You can give it back to him. I have money, or my father does. And Ed can buy anything he likes. Anything I like."

He shook his head. "That's a lovely offer, but I made a deal. I can't go back on it. And I really need to be on my way." He paused. "I could always stop by on the return trip."

She smiled and snuggled closer. "I suppose that will have to do." Sunny closed her eyes and let her body relax. For the first time in weeks, she felt content. And for now, that was enough. As for what would happen in the morning, she'd deal with that when the sun came up.

2

WHEN LOGAN WOKE UP the next morning, she was gone. At first, he wondered if it had all been part of some crazy dream. But when he found the two damp towels, he knew it hadn't been.

He pulled on his jeans and ran his fingers through his hair as memories of their night together flooded his brain. A sudden rush of adrenaline washed away the remaining effects of sleep, and he felt energized. Alive. He hated to admit it, but he had needed a night of really great sex.

Logan bent down and picked up the towels, then carefully folded them. It had been great, hadn't it? It was pretty obvious she'd enjoyed herself, and he'd certainly found the experience memorable. He wasn't sure what the protocol was after a night like last night. Should he find her and say goodbye? Or maybe thank her? Or would that be assuming too much?

She'd left his bed, so she must have decided their night together had come to an end. A rap on the campervan door startled him out of his thoughts, and he hurried over and opened it, hoping he'd find Sunny standing on the other side. Ed was waiting with a plate heaped with food.

"Hey," Logan said, rubbing his eyes against the rising sun.

"Morning," Ed replied. "Come on out. I brought you a proper breakfast. I stopped by earlier, but you didn't answer my knock."

Logan crawled down the stairs and sat on the top step, then took the plate from Ed. It was loaded with eggs and sausage and two slices of toast. He dug in, and a few seconds later, Ed handed him a mug of coffee.

"Thanks. I really need this."

"Didn't sleep well?"

He glanced up and forced a smile. "No, just fine. Like the dead."

"I had one of the stable boys feed and groom Tally. She's all ready to go as soon as you are. I won't bother you with another offer, but if this falls through, make sure I'm the next guy you call, all right?"

"Thanks," Logan said. "Thanks for everything."

Ed held out a piece of paper. "And I called a few breeders and vets that we do business with. You're welcome to stop at any of them if the drive works out right. They'll take good care of you and the filly."

Logan took a deep breath, then grabbed the paper and scanned the five names. "I don't know what to say."

"Why don't you just finish your breakfast? I'll get one of the boys to load Tally, and you can get on the road. And on your way back, make sure you stop. We'll go out for a pint or two."

He thought about the promise he'd made to Sunny. "That would be great. I'll do that." Logan paused. "And if you see Sunny, can you tell her I'm sorry I wasn't able to sell her my horse?"

Ed's brow shot up. "You met Sunny?"

"Yesterday. She came out and rode Tally in the paddock. She offered to buy her and I told her I'd already made a deal."

Ed chuckled. "If that woman didn't have horse sense, she'd have no sense at all. She's right about the filly. I'll give her that."

"Is she always like that? I mean, a little…?"

"We don't call her crazy. She's high-spirited. But I guess I don't blame her. She kind of raised herself, from what I hear. Not much input from the parentals. But she's a helluva rider. She went to the Olympics in London. Show jumping."

"Really? Oh, my God, she's that Sunny Grant. I didn't make the connection."

"She fell apart, knocked out in the early rounds.

She's been hiding out here since then. The media has been brutal."

"That's too bad," Logan said, his mind occupied with thoughts of Sunny and that tiny glimmer of vulnerability he'd seen in her eyes. He knew her intimately, yet he really knew nothing about her life at all. Now that he had a few more pieces, Logan wished he could have had more time with her. Who knows what else he might have discovered?

He finished his breakfast as one of Ed's grooms loaded Tally into the trailer. Logan checked her before he closed the trailer doors, then grabbed his shirt and boots and finished dressing. He'd dragged his departure out as long as he could, hoping he'd see Sunny again. But in the end, Logan had to accept that there would be no goodbye between them.

He got behind the wheel and steered the campervan around the stable and past the house. He glanced over, wondering what she was doing, imagining her lying in bed, her naked body tangled in the sheets. He smiled to himself and headed for the highway.

The next hour was spent rerunning the previous night in his head. It had been a long time since he'd been with a woman. He lived a quiet life on the farm, just him and his right-hand man, Billy. Occasionally, he'd spend a weekend in town, and when he got lucky, there'd be a woman willing to give him a second look.

Since he'd left his job as a banker five years ago,

women just didn't find him as attractive. Funny how a nice guy looked a lot nicer when he had big money. He'd used all his savings, liquidated all his investments to buy the ranch and good breeding stock.

The dream was worth the risk, he'd told himself. And when he'd walked away from the bank on his last day of work, he'd pulled off his tie and unbuttoned his shirt and realized that he was a free man, a man who would determine his own destiny.

Now was not the time to start doubting himself. He had never assumed it would be easy. But the one thing he never realized was how lonely it would be. Logan reached over and slid a CD into the player, then turned up the volume on an old AC/DC tune. He sang along with the song, keeping time with his fist on the steering wheel.

"What time is it?"

The sound of her voice over the song caused him to swerve, and Logan cursed as he brought the campervan and horse trailer back under control. He glanced over his shoulder to see Sunny leaning off the edge of the upper bunk, her pale hair tumbled around her face.

He turned down the music. "What the hell—What are you doing?"

"I was sleeping," she said. She stretched her arms above her head, the sheet dropping away to reveal her naked breasts. "What time is it?"

"What the hell are you—" He turned his attention back to the road and carefully pulled off onto the edge of the highway. Logan turned off the ignition, then stood up. "What the hell are you doing here?"

She frowned. "I decided to come with you. I packed my things and came back, but you were spread across the bed. So I crawled up here and fell asleep." She dragged the sheet around her bare body.

"No, you left. Sometime in the middle of the night."

"Yes, but I came back."

Logan raked his hand through his hair, shaking his head. "Oh, bloody hell. We're two hours gone from your place. I'm going to have to take you back now."

She swung her legs over the edge of the bunk and shrugged. "No. I'm not going back. Nobody cares whether I'm there or not. My father decided to extend his stay in Sydney and won't be home for another month. So I'm going with you. I don't have anything better to do." She jumped down from the bunk and moved toward him, smoothing her palm against his cheek as she passed. She paused and brushed a kiss across his mouth. "Morning," she murmured with a coy smile.

Logan groaned. "This is just what I need right now."

"No reason to get narky," she said, putting on a pout. "I decided I needed more time to convince you to sell me the filly."

"Oh, really. That's why you're running away from home?"

She stared at him for a long moment. "Well, not entirely. But I don't want to talk about that right now. Besides, we'll have fun. I make a very agreeable traveling companion."

The night's activities flashed through his mind and, with a soft curse, Logan slipped his arm around her waist and pulled her against him. Their lips met in a long, deep kiss, and he felt her warm body melt into his. He couldn't say that he was angry or even surprised. He'd known Sunny Grant for less than a day and he already knew she was the most unpredictable woman he'd ever met.

"Won't someone notice you're gone?" he murmured.

"They won't care." She stepped back and ran her fingers through her hair. "I need coffee." She glanced down at the sheet wrapped around her body. "Can we stop somewhere?"

"I think you should get dressed," he said. "Did you bring clothes?"

"Yes," she said. "And money." She reached up and dug through her bag, pulling out her purse. But after rummaging through it, she looked up. "Oh, no."

"What?"

"I don't have money. I must have taken my wallet out of my purse and I was half-asleep when I packed and—"

"Don't worry, I have money."

"I'll pay you back. I can call Lily, our house-keeper, and she can send me some. I'm a really cheap date."

"I find that very hard to believe," he muttered.

She smiled at him, then crawled into the passenger seat, tucking her feet beneath the sheet. "I like this. It'll be a little adventure. God knows I needed to get out of that house."

"A little adventure," he repeated. With Sunny Grant in tow, that was the understatement of the day.

Logan slipped behind the wheel and started the campervan, then carefully pulled back out onto the highway. He stole a glance over at her and found her watching him. "What?"

"Nothing," she said. "I'm just glad you didn't put me out on the highway."

"I wouldn't have done that," Logan said. "Maybe if you had shoes and clothes on I might have considered it. But dressed in just a sheet, you would have been at a disadvantage."

"Well, thank you for that," she said.

"Am I going to be sorry I let you stay?"

She grinned. "I don't know." Her smiled faded and she drew in a deep breath. "But if you really don't want me here, I can find my way home."

For a moment, she looked so sad, and he wondered what would bring such sorrow to that beautiful face. Logan groaned inwardly. He would have plenty of time to figure her all out. From here to Perth was a long drive. "No," he said. "I think we'll be fine."

SUNNY STOOD IN FRONT of the refrigerated section in the supermarket. Logan had given her thirty dollars and a half hour to buy whatever snacks and drinks she needed. She'd never done much shopping for food. That was usually left up to their housekeeper. But there were certain things that she liked.

She glanced down at the money she held in her hand. Though he didn't come right out and say it, it was clear to Sunny that Logan didn't have a lot of extra cash, especially to spend on food for her. As she wandered the store, she'd been trying to figure out a way to get some money of her own, but she wasn't really sure where they'd be stopping or when they'd get there.

It felt strange to be living in the real world, where money dominated almost every decision. Throughout her life, she'd never had to worry about how to pay the bills. Her father had handed her a bank card when she'd turned thirteen and there were never any questions asked about what she used it for.

"Are you almost done?"

She saw Logan's reflection in the glass door then spun around. "Sorry." She pulled out a couple of bottles of orange juice and put them in the shopping basket.

"Is that all?" he asked.

"Yes."

He reached inside and grabbed a few more, then took some bottled water, as well. "We're not going to find a lot of places to stop once we head west. I'm going to get some ice. Pick out some snacks. Maybe something for sandwiches."

Sunny found some packaged ham and sliced cheese, then searched the store for bread. Along the way she grabbed a few packages of crisps and then decided a bottle of wine might come in handy. By the time Logan returned with the ice, she'd spent her thirty dollars.

As they walked to the checkout, he examined her purchases, then pointed to the wine. "Maybe you should have gotten another bottle," he said.

"One is enough for now," she said with a smile.

"I'm not used to traveling with women. Is there anything else that you need? Lipstick? Nail polish?"

"I remembered my toothbrush," she said. "But I forgot shampoo. I can use yours, I guess."

He stopped. "I'll get some for you and meet you in the queue."

When he returned, he set the shampoo down next to her purchases. "I'd rather not smell my shampoo in your hair. This smells like grapefruit."

Sunny opened the bottle and took a sniff. "Mmm. That's nice."

The checkout operator was watching them closely, and she turned to Logan, awaiting his next comment.

He cursed beneath his breath, then nodded. "We're done. Add it up."

"Are you sure?" the checkout operator asked.

"Add it up," Sunny said. She grabbed a package of Tim Tams from a rack and put it next to the shampoo. "Women need chocolate, too."

They walked back to the campervan, and Logan opened the passenger door for her. Sunny jumped in and settled herself into the now familiar spot. A few seconds later, Logan got behind the wheel.

"Thank you," she murmured. "I do intend to pay you back."

"No worries," he murmured.

"I'm wondering if I might arrange to have some money sent to me. If we pick a town down the road, I can have it sent there. But I'm not sure where we're going next."

"We're not going to have a lot of time for shopping. I know you're used to luxuries—"

"No," she murmured. "I just don't want to be a burden. In fact, from now on, I'm not going to eat at all. Unless you let me arrange for my own money, I'm going to fast for the rest of the trip."

"Don't be ridiculous. You have to eat."

"I don't have to do anything I don't want to do," she said. "I'll eat my Tim Tams. I can make those last at least three days."

"Oh, Jaysus," he said, leaning over the steering wheel and bumping his head against the top edge.

"I should probably kill myself now." He drew a deep breath, then reached down and grabbed his mobile phone from one of the cup holders. "Have at it."

"Where?"

He pulled out the map and traced their route. From Brisbane they'd head west, into the interior of New South Wales on A2, then southwest to the coast again. He pointed to Adelaide. "There. We'll be there day after tomorrow. Have it sent to a local bank."

"Cool," she said. Sunny dialed her home number and when Lily answered, she quickly explained her dilemma. In the end, the housekeeper agreed to express her wallet and credit cards to her father's business office in Adelaide. After spending a few days on the road in the campervan, she'd treat Logan to a comfortable bed and a hot shower.

"All right," she said to Lily as she scribbled down the office address. "And if it's not too much trouble, can you just gather a few nice things for me to wear? Some summer dresses. And my lavender-scented lotion? And—" Sunny paused. She'd learned to do without the creature comforts. She could certainly last a little longer. "That's all." She hung up and handed the phone to Logan, who was watching her suspiciously. "What?"

"Lavender-scented lotion? Is that what you were wearing last night?"

She nodded. "It's my favorite. And it's really hard to find. It's French."

"I like the way you smell," he said.

Sunny crawled out of her seat and settled herself on top of him, her backside wedged against the steering wheel. Wrapping her arms around his neck, she bent close and gave him a long, deep kiss. " We're going to have fun. I promise."

He smoothed his hands beneath her shirt, sliding his palm along her torso until he cupped her breast. She wasn't wearing a bra. "Maybe we should have bought you some underwear."

"I brought underwear," she said. "I just don't like to wear it. It gets in the way."

"Of what?"

"Of your hands on my body," she whispered. Sunny bent close and brushed her lips across his, teasing with the tip of her tongue. A tiny smile curled the corners of his mouth. Though she was just getting to know him, she'd already decided he was the sweetest guy she'd ever met.

He was so humble and genuine and he didn't try to be anything but himself. She'd known far too many men who spent their energy trying to impress. He had a quiet confidence that she found incredibly attractive.

For a long moment, they lost themselves in the kiss, Sunny wriggling against him until he groaned in protest. But then a loud bang interrupted them and they turned to see a security guard standing outside the driver's-side door.

"Move along now, folks," he said.

Sunny giggled as she crawled back to her own seat. Logan started the ignition and slowly pulled out of the parking lot. She opened the box of biscuits and slowly munched on one as she watched the traffic.

"Are you going to offer me one of those or are you going to eat them all yourself?" Logan asked.

"I was thinking about eating them all by myself. Why, do you want one?"

"I could eat one," he said.

"I'll give you one if you answer a question," she said.

"What kind of question?"

"A personal question. Before last night, when was the last time you were with a woman?"

"Tim Tam first," he said, holding out his hand. Sunny gave him one of the biscuits. "I had a beer at the local pub the night before I left and I believe Becky Pelson was the barkeep."

"You slept with the barkeep?"

"No, you asked when I was last with a woman. As I recall, she was the last until I met you."

"Oh! Waste of a Tim Tam! You cheat."

"I can't be held accountable for your poor phrasing," he said with a grin. "If you give me another biscuit, I'll answer the question."

She handed him a Tim Tam. "Honest answer."

"It's been a while," he said. "Probably about six months. I'm not sure, exactly."

"You don't have a woman in your life, then?"

He glanced over at her. "No. I wouldn't have spent the night with you if I had. I'm not that kind of bloke."

"I know," Sunny said. "I can tell that about you. You're one of the good ones." She handed him another biscuit.

"Will you answer a question from me?"

Sunny nodded. She knew what he'd probably ask, but for some reason she wasn't afraid to reveal anything to this man. They had a lot of kilometers in front of them and plenty of time to get to know each other. She wasn't sure what would happen at the end of the trip, but there was no reason to play games. "All right."

"Was it me that you wanted last night or were you just looking for a warm body?"

"It was you. When we were standing by the fence watching Tally, you were nice and you didn't judge me. I was just really tired of people judging me."

"Why would they judge you?"

"Because of what happened in London?"

She didn't see any change in his expression. "Ed told me about it. Everyone has bad days, Sunny."

"Well, I picked a very bad day to have a bad day. Washed out of the qualifying round in show jumping. I was supposed to win a gold medal. Instead, I embarrassed myself, my horse, my father, all my coaches and the entire country."

"You're human," Logan said.

"Yeah. I keep telling myself that, but it doesn't make me feel any better."

He pointed to the package of biscuits. "You want to ask more questions? I'm still hungry."

As they headed west, they traded questions, learning more about each other with each kilometer that passed. And with their lighthearted conversation, Sunny was able to put her troubles behind her and just relax. There were no expectations between them beyond an enjoyment of the scenery that passed and the company they kept.

THEY STOPPED FOR the night near Moree, a small town in the heart of the black soil plains. Ed had given him the name of a local veterinarian who'd worked at one of the equestrian centers in Brisbane before starting a practice of his own. He had a spare stable for Tally, and once she was fed and bedded down, Logan unhitched the trailer, and he and Sunny headed into town.

They bought dinner from a Thai restaurant, then found a small park along the river, sitting at a picnic table near the water. They opened the bottle of wine Sunny had purchased and shared the prawns and noodles, eating with the single fork that he had in the campervan.

She'd changed into a pretty cotton dress, her arms bare and her body beneath the same. He couldn't help but think about how simple it would be to pull the dress over her head to reveal her silken skin.

He'd tried not to let himself become infatuated, but there was just something about her he found irresistible. It was so easy to forget that they'd just met. Already, there was an ease between them, as if they'd been friends for years.

Though he'd known a lot of women, he'd never really been able to figure them out. But Sunny was like an open book to him. He could look at her and tell exactly what she was thinking. Not that she really kept her thoughts to herself. She had an opinion about everything, from his driving to his taste in Thai food to the way he wore his hat.

Logan stretched his legs out in front of him and took a long sip of his wine. He reached over and slipped his fingers through the hair at her nape, then pulled her into a quick kiss. "I'm glad you fell asleep in that bunk. I'm having a lot more fun than I ever thought I'd have on this trip."

"I thought I annoyed you," she said.

"No. You don't annoy me."

Sunny took a bite of the noodles and stared out at the river. "Do you really want to sell her?" she asked.

Logan took a deep breath and shook his head. How many times were they going to talk about this? "No, but I really don't have a choice. Sometimes you're forced to make the hard decisions. If I want to keep my ranch, I have to sell her. And that's what my business is, Sunny. Raising and selling horses. If I get attached to every horse I raise, I'm not going to make any money."

"She should be ridden. And trained for the ring. She's big and beautiful, too beautiful to use just for breeding. I could make something of her. I could train her."

"I assume she will be ridden," he said, forcing a smile. "It's fine. She's going to a good place. And I'm glad you decided to come along. If you weren't here to distract me, I'd probably be a basket case by the time I got to Perth."

"How long have you had your ranch?"

"Five years. I used to make big money as an investment banker. I worked real hard for four years and saved all my money to buy the ranch. It isn't much, but it's mine. And the bank's."

"I can't imagine you in a suit and tie," she said. Her brow furrowed into a frown. "Wait. Give me a second. All right, yes I can. I bet you were quite the handsome man."

"I am quite the man now," he said. "Even without the suit and tie."

She handed him the carton of noodles and took a sip from her own wine. "You know what I'd like to do? I'd like to find a spot where we could park and build a campfire. I saw a sign for a caravan park. We could get a spot and maybe they'd have a shower?"

"I think we can do that," he said. He'd been wondering about finding them a motel room for the night, but camping sounded like much more fun. "Grab the wine. Let's find a spot."

When they got back out to the street, they found the sign and followed it to a large caravan park on the south side of the town. The park featured a special attraction in the town of Moree—hot mineral springs and thermal baths.

"Oh, that sounds wonderful," Sunny said. "Now I wish I had my bikini. I wonder if Lily has sent my things yet."

"I'm sure they probably have a spare that you could borrow," Logan said.

They paid the fee for the site and got things set up, hooking up to the power and opening all the windows to the late-evening breeze.

It was almost nine when they strolled over to the thermal pools. The park was quiet. It was still early in the season and the middle of the week, so the campground was nearly empty. Sunny sat down on the edge of one of the smaller pools and pulled off her shoes, then let her legs dangle in the hot water.

She looked up at him with a smile. "I feel healthier already. I think I'm going to have to go in."

"Do you have anything on under that dress?"

She shook her head. "Nope. But no one will see. It's dark and there's no one around."

"Did you bring anything you could swim in?"

"I suppose I could just wear my underwear."

Sunny grinned at him. "Would you go get my underwear? I put it in the drawer next to the bed."

He pointed at her, giving her a warning glare. "Leave that dress on until I get back."

Logan strode back to the campervan. Once inside, he picked through the skimpy bits of lingerie that Sunny had bothered to bring with her. There was nothing even remotely close to a bikini amongst the lace and silk panties and bras.

It felt odd picking through her underthings. He barely knew her. In truth, he wasn't even sure what she was to him. His girlfriend? His lover? If he were forced to suddenly define their relationship, he had no idea what he'd say.

Logan picked out a black bra and a pair of red undies that looked as if they'd at least cover part of her bum. When he got back to the thermal pool, he noticed her dress, tossed into a heap beside the water. "I thought I told you to wait," he said.

She turned and folded her arms on the edge of the deck. "I couldn't. The water looked so nice. And we're all alone here."

Logan's gaze drifted along her naked body, the sweet curves of her backside, her slender legs barely hidden by the rippling water. He'd been in a heightened state of desire all afternoon and evening, just barely able to contain himself whenever he touched her or even looked at her. But now, seeing her body, so incredibly beautiful and distracting, he felt his desire bubble over into a very distinct reaction.

"Put these on," he said, holding out the bra and undies.

"Don't be a prude, no one can see me."

"I can see you," he said.

A wicked grin curled the corners of her mouth. "I want you to see me. I'm actually trying to seduce you."

"Yeah? Well, I'd have to be an idiot not to realize that."

"Come in," she said. "The water feels wonderful." She held out her hand and he caught a glimpse of her naked breasts. "Wear your underdaks if you don't want to get naked."

He held out the lingerie then dropped them into the water. "I'll come in when you put those on."

Reluctantly, she pulled the undies on, then struggled with the bra. "I could use some help."

He squatted down next to the pool and, with fumbling fingers, he hooked the back of the bra. Touching her sent a current through his body, setting every nerve buzzing. Smoothing his hands over her shoulders, he leaned close and pressed his lips to the curve of her neck.

She spun around and floated away from him, watching him from the far side of the small, round pool. "Come on," she said.

Logan glanced around. What the hell…the place

was practically empty. He tugged his T-shirt over his head, skimmed his cargo shorts over his hips, kicked off his trainers and stepped down into the warm water. Her gaze fixed on his crotch, on the growing erection that pressed against the soft fabric of his underdaks.

"You're trouble," he murmured, sinking down into the pool.

She came over to him and slipped her arms around his neck. "Isn't that exactly what you're looking for?" she asked. Sunny wrapped her legs around his waist, then kissed him, her lips lush and ripe, the taste of her like the most exotic fruit.

He'd never put much thought into kissing. It was a great way to lure a girl into bed, but beyond that, it was nothing more than foreplay. But now Logan realized that he'd just never been kissed by Sunny Grant. Like everything she did, she kissed with reckless abandon, holding nothing back.

"Isn't this where we started?" he murmured.

"No," she responded. "We started in the paddock with that beautiful horse."

"We did?"

She nodded. "From the first moment I saw you, I was…interested."

"When did you decide to seduce me?"

"When I saw you staring at my ass," she teased. "I knew you were seducible."

"And now? You better have something planned for me now, Sunny."

She boosted herself up on the edge of the pool and motioned him over. "Turn around and sit." When he did, Sunny began to massage his shoulders. "You really should let me do some of the driving. You wouldn't get so tense."

"Hauling a trailer is a lot harder than it seems," he said, tipping his head. "Oh, now, that feels fine. Right there."

Sunny continued to work at the knots in his neck and shoulders, and he lost himself in the feel of her hands on his body. When he was completely relaxed, she slipped back into the water and sank down in front of him.

She reached down to touch his shaft. Logan sucked in a sharp breath and watched her. Her touch was like a powerful narcotic, making him forget all truth and reason, bringing him to the point of complete surrender.

"I'm not sure that the managers are going to appreciate what we're doing in their pool," he whispered.

"I'm sure people have done worse," she said, grinning. A moment later, she submerged and ran her tongue along the length of him, before bobbing back to the surface and sending him a wicked smile. Then, she floated away from him and stepped out of the pool. "Are you going to come?"

"I think I'm just going to sit here for a spell. I don't want to embarrass myself if we run into any other campers."

"Suit yourself," she murmured. Grabbing her dress, she turned and walked toward their site, the water from her hair running down her body, her skin gleaming. Logan groaned softly when she reached back to unhook her bra.

Wincing, he got out of the water and snatched up his clothes, holding them in front of him. When he got back to the campervan, he noticed that the lights inside had been turned off. He opened the door and stepped inside, and in an instant, she pinned him against the wall.

Grabbing his clothes from his hands, Sunny tossed them aside, then twisted her fingers in the waistband of his underdaks and pulled them down over his hips. He barely had time to take a breath before he felt her warm mouth on his rigid shaft.

A gasp slipped from his lips and he braced his hands on the back of the passenger seat, stunned by the wash of sensation that nearly overwhelmed him. Logan closed his eyes, his body dancing on the edge of sublime surrender.

Holding his breath, he tried to regain control, to focus on something other than what her lips and tongue were doing to him. His heart slammed in his chest and the world seemed to blur all around him. The need to surrender could only be denied for so long. And when he finally felt that he'd reached his limit, she slowly stood, then pulled him over to the bed.

He quickly stripped off the lacy undies, tossing them to the floor. When they fell onto the bed, their bodies met, skin against skin, limbs tangling. It was as if she were made just for him, every perfect part of her designed for his touch alone.

And when she sheathed him and he buried himself deep inside her, Logan knew that there was something extraordinary happening between them. The most improbable emotions surged up inside of him as he looked down into her beautiful face. He'd known her for a day, yet he was already hopelessly infatuated with her. And to his complete and utter surprise, he wasn't afraid to admit it to himself.

Though all of this would come to an end in a few weeks, for now, Logan was going to enjoy Sunny while he could.

3

SUNNY SAT DOWN on the edge of the bed, then leaned over and pressed a kiss to Logan's shoulder. She loved to watch him while he slept. There was a perfect peace about him, so different from the simmering energy he gave off when he was awake.

She wondered if she'd ever really know what went on inside his head. Usually, she had a man figured out by the time he took her to bed. Most of the men she knew had been a simple mix of ego and desire, satisfied to have one need stroked, ecstatic to have both tended to.

But Logan kept his ego in check. And she was just beginning to understand the depths of his desire. For him, it wasn't just about physical pleasure. When they were in the midst of making love, theirs was a deeper connection, a bond that grew stronger with every minute they spent together.

She stared down into his face, carefully taking in each perfect feature. He was a virtual stranger, and yet she felt as if she'd known him her whole life. If she weren't so cynical about love, she might actually believe that was what she was feeling. But after watching her parents' marriage fall apart, she'd vowed never to indulge in that particular emotion. This was just an infatuation, a wonderful, playful crush that would probably end the moment their trip did.

Sunny sighed. As romantic as this little getaway was, she'd do well to keep it all in perspective. Sure, he made her feel good about herself—he made her believe there was at least one person in the world who really cared about her.

But she'd been with other men. And she'd always found a way to destroy whatever affections they'd had for her when she grew bored or frustrated with the relationship. Though she couldn't imagine that happening with Logan, her own history told her the time would come just as sure as night followed day.

Sunny held the cup of coffee near his nose and softly called his name. "Wake up," she said. "Time to get up."

He opened one eye, then the other, and pushed up on his arm. "You got coffee?"

"I took some money out of your wallet. I hope you don't mind."

He raked his hand through his rumpled hair. "No.

Well done, you." Taking the covered paper cup from her hand, he leaned over and dropped a kiss on her lips. "Morning."

"Good morning. You slept well."

"I did," he said. "Thanks to you and that massage you gave me. I was knackered after all our activities."

Sunny reached out and brushed a strand of hair from his eyes. "You needed the exercise. After sitting on your arse all day."

"I do appreciate that you're watching out for me."

The coffee was strong, and Sunny sipped at it as she glanced around the interior of the campervan. "You know, this wouldn't be such a bad place to live. I mean, if you got it all fitted out and bought some supplies. You could just travel all around, see things you never saw."

"I'm not sure a girl like you would be comfortable living out of a campervan."

She frowned. "Why not?"

He paused. "I'd think you'd want the comforts of home. Running water, hot showers? A big soft bed."

"Those kinds of things don't make you happy."

"What does make you happy, Sunny?" he asked.

She wanted to admit that it was him, but her feelings were still too new to believe in them. "Good coffee," she said. "And a hot man. Or is it hot coffee and a good man?"

He sat up and crossed his legs in front of him, pulling the sheet over his lap. "I used to live in this campervan. When I first bought the ranch, the house was a wreck. The roof leaked, there were birds living in the kitchen. It took me quite a while to make it habitable."

"I'd like to see your place sometime," she said.

He smiled tightly. "Sure. Sometime."

"I mean it."

"It's nothing like your place, Sunny. You live in a castle, I live in a cardboard box."

"Are you really that preoccupied with money?"

"I'm practical. And realistic. Money makes everything easier. It buys access, it smooths the way, it provides comfort and security. You can't deny that, can you?"

She shook her head. He was right. She'd always taken her father's wealth for granted. Having every little need catered to had turned her into a vapid and self-centered child. When she looked in the mirror lately, she didn't really like what she saw—a woman with nothing to call her own.

Sunny stood up. "All right, then. Perhaps later we can talk about religion or politics."

He grabbed her hand and pulled her back down on the bed, capturing her mouth in a long, sweet kiss. Maybe she wasn't sure who she was. But she knew who Logan thought she was, and seeing herself through his eyes made her feel better about herself. He wanted her, he needed her, and she got the sense that he might just be falling for her.

"We should probably get on the road," he said. "We still have to pick up Tally from the vet's place. And we've got a long day ahead. I want to get to Cobar tonight, and with a long drive tomorrow, we'll be able to reach Adelaide. Ed gave me the name of a horse breeder about an hour outside Adelaide. I'm thinking we might stay a few days and give Tally a chance to recover a bit."

"All right, let's get going," Sunny murmured, her lips soft against his mouth.

"Or maybe we could go back to bed for a bit."

"Are you saying I wasn't enough for you last night?" she asked.

"I'm saying I'm never going to get enough of you, no matter how much time we spend in bed."

She set her coffee cup down and flopped back on the bed with him, turning to face him and look into his eyes. "Tell me the truth," she said, nerves twisting and tightening deep inside her.

"The truth," he said.

"Do you think less of me because we…because I seduced you without even knowing you?"

"No," he said, cupping her face in his hands. He brushed a kiss across her lips. "No, not at all. I wanted to be with you. But I'm not sure I would have had the courage to make the first move."

"You don't think I'm…you know…the village bike?"

He chuckled. "No. I thought you were a woman

who knew what she wanted and wasn't afraid to go after it. And I still think that about you. You're not afraid to live life, Sunny. And when I'm around you, I'm not afraid, either."

"You're a very kind man, Logan Quinn."

"And you're a very beautiful woman, Sunny Grant."

They came together for a long, sweet kiss, Logan dragging her body against his, his hands searching for bare skin beneath her T-shirt. When he found her breast, he teased at her nipple with his thumb, drawing to a hard peak. Sunny closed her eyes and moaned softly.

What was it about this man that made him so irresistible? He was real and true, possessed of an inner resolve that she found so admirable, the kind of man a woman could depend upon.

When she was a teenager, she'd dreamed about her own personal Prince Charming, a man who would rescue her from all of her fears and insecurities. But as she grew older, the cynicism began to set in. She saw the worst that love could become in her parents' horrible marriage and she stopped believing in fairy-tale endings.

But maybe she'd given up too soon. She was only twenty-six. That was far too early to harden her heart. "Come on," she said. "The sooner we leave, the sooner we get where we're going."

"Maybe I don't want this trip to end," he said.

Sunny crawled off the bunk and grabbed her coffee, then slipped into her spot in the passenger seat. She pulled out the map. "How long is this trip?"

He followed her off the bed, standing in the middle of the campervan completely naked. The sight of his perfect body sent a delicious shiver through her. "From here? About four thousand kilometers. When we get to Adelaide, we'll be about halfway there, give or take a few hundred kilometers." He reached down to pick up his shorts.

"Stop," she said.

He glanced up. "Stop?"

"Just let me look before you put your clothes on. It's going to be a while before you take them off again."

He chuckled. "Once we get out of town, I could strip down and drive starkers if that would please you."

"Oh, yes," she said. "That would be lovely."

With a laugh, he pulled on his shorts and a T-shirt, and found a pair of trainers for his feet. Then he slipped behind the wheel.

"What, no underdaks?" she asked.

"If you refuse to wear knickers, then so can I."

Sunny leaned over and kissed his cheek, then pointed out the windscreen. "Once more into the breach, dear friend," she cried.

"Shakespeare. *Henry the Fifth,* isn't it?"

"Yes." Sunny paused. "'There's nothing so becomes a man as modest stillness and humility.'" It was the perfect description of him, she mused.

"All right," he said, glancing over at her. "Prepare to be schooled. I happen to be a Shakespeare expert. I've got his complete works somewhere in this campervan."

"We had to memorize all kinds of quotes in high school," she said.

"The benefits of a posh private school?"

"Hey, I learned how to kiss boys and smoke cigarettes in private school."

He grinned. "All right then. I'll want to be hearing about that a bit later."

THE DAY'S DRIVE HAD been long, the past two hours south of Bourke spent on a narrow strip of sealed road that cut a straight line through the Aussie outback.

They pulled into Cobar at seven in the evening and found another caravan park. But this time, they kept Tally with them. Once they had their site, Sunny helped Logan take her out of the trailer. He attached a long lead to the filly and Sunny patiently exercised the filly on an expanse of grass, softly speaking to her as the horse made a wide circle around her.

It was easy to forget that they shared a love of horses, but now, watching her work with Tally, he had to admire how she focused on the task at hand. He was seeing a whole different side of her, not the brazen sex goddess that he'd come to know from their nights together, but a professional, with a depth of knowledge much greater than his own.

He was sorry he hadn't called Ed first when he'd decided he'd have to sell the filly. He could have almost handled parting with her if he knew the horse was going to someone like Sunny. She would love and appreciate Tally as much as he did.

"Look how beautiful she is," Sunny called. "It's like she's got feathers for feet. I'd love to see her jump. Have you trained her at all?"

He shook his head. "No."

"She just looks so graceful. I hope your buyer appreciates what he's getting."

He watched them silently. Why not just sell her the horse? His loss would at least be tempered by the knowledge that the filly was in the best possible hands. But he wasn't even sure how to back out of the deal. Papers had been signed, money had been exchanged.

He'd taken a third, eight thousand dollars, as a down payment, but that had already gone to paying bills at the ranch. He had nothing to return to the buyer. Logan shook his head. Never mind the fact that he was driving across Australia to deliver her.

"I saw a restaurant just down the road," Logan said. "I'm going to walk over and grab us something for supper. Is there anything special you'd like?"

"A cheeseburger," she said. "And a chocolate malt.

And see if they have pie. Or cake. Something yummy for dessert. And a bag of crisps would be good, too. I think we finished the crisps this afternoon."

"That all?"

"Biscuits for my horse," she said.

"Your horse?"

She glanced over her shoulder. "I can dream, can't I?"

"I have biscuits in the trailer," he said.

"That's all, then," she said, shooting him a smile. "Hurry back."

The street was quiet as he walked over to the restaurant, a slight chill in the air. He drew a deep breath and looked up at the first stars twinkling in the midnight-blue sky.

Of all the things he'd expected on this trip, Sunny hadn't even been a glimmer in his mind. And here she was, the best traveling companion he could have hoped for. He felt content, completely satisfied by life. And one of the hardest things he'd have to do— selling Tally—would be made easier by her presence.

The roadside restaurant was nearly empty when Logan entered. He sat down at the counter and grabbed a menu, then recited the order for the waitress. He had a cup of coffee while he waited, taking the time to think back over the events of the day.

He'd never been on a family holiday. His parents had never had the extra money to waste on a special trip. Occasionally, his mother would take Logan and his younger brother somewhere exciting. Once they spent the day at the zoo and another day on the beach. He imagined that his road trip with Sunny might be something like the typical family holiday.

They'd sung songs to each other and played trivia games, they'd told silly childhood stories, and she'd quoted Shakespeare from the book she found in campervan. And then, there were times when they were just quiet, watching the scenery pass by, lost in their own thoughts.

The waitress delivered their dinner, packed in two paper sacks. They still had cold drinks in the cooler, purchased along the route that day. He got to the door, then remembered Sunny's request for dessert and returned to the counter. "How much for the rest of that chocolate cake?" he asked.

"You want a half a cake?" the waitress asked, eyebrows raised.

Logan nodded. "My girlfriend loves chocolate."

"I don't know. There's probably six pieces there. I'd say twelve dollars?"

He laid out the cash and waited as she packed the cake into a box, then tied it with a string. It wasn't much, but he knew it would please her. And for some reason, he felt the need to do that more often. Wasn't that part of romance, making those tiny gestures?

When he got back to the caravan park, Tally was grazing on a clump of hay out of the rack on the side of the trailer. Sunny had filled a bucket of water and clipped it next to the hay. The horse looked up at him as he passed, blinking silently. "You're a pretty girl," he said.

The lights were on inside the campervan, and music drifted out from the CD player. He looked through the door to see Sunny straightening up the small galley kitchen. He knocked on the door and she turned and smiled.

"Honey, I'm home."

A tiny giggle slipped from her lips and she opened the door for him and stepped aside. "Hello, honey, how was your day?"

"Oh, honey, it was wonderful. How was your day?"

"Just lovely," she said. "Now give me my cheeseburger. I'm famished."

They sat down at the table and spread the food out in front of them, sharing the chocolate malt between them. When that was gone, Logan fetched a couple of beers, removing the caps before setting the bottles on the table.

"I talked to the park manager. They don't treat the grass here, so we can let Tally graze."

"Great," he said.

"I noticed there was an old saddle in the trailer. I was thinking I might get up early tomorrow, before we have to leave, and put her through her paces. Would that be all right with you?"

Logan nodded. "Just don't get too attached to her."

"I won't," Sunny said. "I know she's meant for someone else."

In a different life, he might have been able to make a gift of the horse. What would it be like to have that kind of financial freedom? He'd already had doubts that he could make the ranch work. There were times when all the scrimping and saving just wore him out.

"How many horses to do you have on your ranch?"

"I started with six mares and I have twenty-six now. I breed them artificially."

"We do, too. Although we own the three stallions that we use for that. It's sad that the mares never get to enjoy that particular pleasure."

"Pleasure?"

Sunny grinned. "Yeah, I know, it isn't a pretty sight when they do it the natural way." She took a bite of her cheeseburger. "Thank goodness, humans know how to do it better."

He chuckled softly. "Thank goodness."

They lingered over the meal, chatting about Logan's ranch and his theories about horse breeding. He imagined this was what it would be like to have a woman in his life full-time. Meals together, companionship, mind-blowing sex and someone there to back him up, to make him feel as if life wasn't as bad as it sometimes looked.

When they were finished, he helped Sunny clean up the table then watched her from the sofa as she sorted through her clothes and neatly folded them. "What time do we have to leave tomorrow?"

"Early. I'd like to get to the breeder's place before dark. And then, I was thinking we could find a place to stay for the night. Maybe near a beach?"

"So, we don't have to go to bed right now," Sunny said. "We can have a little fun?"

"What kind of fun can we have in Cobar?"

She held out her hand, then pulled him to his feet. "It's not what you do, it's who you're with."

The moment he touched her, he couldn't help but draw her into his arms and kiss her. It had become such a natural part of their life together. Kissing and touching. He couldn't imagine how he'd go on without having her beside him.

Logan knew the realities of their relationship already. They'd have a beginning and a very definite ending. When their trip was over, he'd go back to his life and she'd return to hers. No matter how he looked at it, they couldn't exist in the same world. Sunny wasn't cut out to live in the middle of nowhere and he wasn't going to settle into her life, living among the tall poppies.

"What are we doing?" he asked as she leaned over to turn up the music.

"We're dancing," she said.

He gasped. "You might be dancing, but don't include me in this. I'm not going to let you turn me into a fool for your own amusement."

"No, I'm not going to make fun. Dancing can be very sexy. It's public foreplay. Everyone should know how to dance." She listened to the music, then shook her head. "This won't do."

She searched the CDs but finally settled on a radio station. A soft instrumental tune came through the speakers and she glanced over her shoulder at him. "There. See?"

Sunny stood in front of him and took his hands. "Now, we'll just sway a little bit, until you get the rhythm of the music."

He drew a deep breath. "Really? I'm not going to be good at this."

"Any man who is as good in bed as you are has to have some kind of rhythm. Now slip your right hand around my waist and pull me a little closer."

"All right, I can get behind that." But when he did, he forgot to keep swaying and he stumbled a bit before getting back into the song.

"Now, hold your left hand out and I'm going to just let my hand rest there."

They continued to move around the cramped interior of the campervan, their bodies coming closer and closer with each verse of the music. To Logan's amazement, he was doing quite well.

"It's like sex," she murmured, her lips brushing against his ear. "You just have to let go and enjoy it."

"What's next?"

"Now we keep doing this. And you whisper sweet

things to me and kiss me and imagine what it would be like to take me to bed."

"I don't have to imagine that."

"But you do," she said. "Because dancing is all about anticipation and patience. Letting the feel of your body against mine play with your senses." She drew back to look into his eyes. "Do you feel it?"

Logan had danced before, but never like this. It was exactly as she said—slow, delicious foreplay. And yet, nothing they were doing was overtly sexual. It was all happening in his imagination. "I do," he said.

They continued to dance, their bodies moving together, a slow burn growing between them. He bent close and captured her mouth with his, and yet the rhythm went on, as if the seduction had a life of its own. And when they finally stumbled to the bed, Logan wasn't sure he'd be able to maintain any control at all.

His mouth covered hers in a deep, almost desperate kiss as they quickly undressed each other. She arched against him as they tumbled onto the bed. Pinning her hands above her head, he slowly entered her, and when he drew back, Logan looked into her eyes, as if reading her response to every move he made.

He knew he ought to get protection, but when he reached for the box of condoms, she shook her head. "I'm all right," she said softly. "If you are…"

They'd been together such a short time, yet he knew he wanted to feel her completely. And it was perfect, a sensation so intense that his body trembled as he tried to maintain control. He knew how to move, exactly how to dictate her responses, how to bring her close and then draw her back from the edge. It was as if their bodies had been meant for each other, designed to give each other pleasure.

He braced himself on his arms, slowing his pace until she could feel every inch of him as he plunged into her moist heat.

Sunny's breathing grew quicker, and he felt her body tensing ever so slightly. And when he was certain that she was as close as he was, he let himself feel it all. A delicious heat spread through him, his body slowly coiling tighter with each stroke. It was a tantalizing ascent, spinning up and up until every nerve in his body was humming.

"Look at me," he whispered.

She moaned, her voice sounding like an echo in his head. He gently bit her lower lip and she opened her eyes. Sunny's breath caught in her throat and, suddenly, she was there, tumbling over the edge.

A cry of surprise tore from her throat as her body dissolved into deep spasms. Their gazes never faltered and he drove into her one more time before joining her in his own powerful orgasm.

The pleasure seemed to go on forever, only abating when they were both completely spent and gasping for breath. Though his arms felt boneless, Logan braced above her and bent closer to kiss her. "Do you know how incredible that feels? To do that together?"

"Mmm," she murmured with a sleepy smile. "We are becoming quite good at it."

He chuckled softly and rolled off her. "You know what they say about practice?"

"What?"

He stretched out beside her, lying on his stomach and toying with a strand of her hair. "It should be done enthusiastically and often."

"I'll remember that," she said with a laugh.

Logan stared at her beautiful face. He wanted to tell her how much she meant to him, how he was falling completely under her spell, but he knew it was too soon. Sunny wasn't the type to want undying proclamations of love and affection. She seemed to be happy when everything was light and carefree.

He ran his fingers over her brow, then dropped a kiss on her lips. For now, he'd play the game by her rules. "I'm going to go put Tally into the trailer for the night."

"I'll come and help you," she said.

"No, you stay here. It'll only take me a minute."

She watched him from the bed as he pulled on a pair of shorts and slipped into his trainers. He noticed the box with the chocolate cake sitting on the counter. "We forgot dessert," he said.

"What?"

Logan grabbed the box and set it down beside her on the bed, then retrieved the single fork they had. "Why don't you get started on that and I'll be back in a few?"

He walked outside into the cool night, quietly closing the screen door behind him. A moment later, he heard a tiny scream and smiled to himself. Sunny was pleased.

Tally gave him a curious look as he approached, the light from the campervan reflected in her eyes. "Don't worry," he murmured. "You're still my best girl."

He rubbed the horse's neck and she nuzzled his shoulder, her soft nose nudging him for a biscuit. He unclipped her from the lead, then walked her back to the trailer. He opened the upper sections of the trailer doors and turned Tally around so she could enjoy the scents on the night air. Then he grabbed a biscuit from the tin and held out his hand.

"One more day on the road," he said as the horse took the biscuit from his palm. "Then I'm going to give you a few days' rest." He fetched her water and put the rest of the hay in the rack, then closed the trailer door. The filly hung her head out and he gave her another biscuit. "Good night, baby."

He walked back to the campervan, and when he got inside, he found Sunny sitting cross-legged in the center of the bed. She pointed the fork at him. "You are the most amazing man I've ever met."

Logan sat down next to her. She fed him a bite of cake and he smiled. "Are you saying that because of the sex or the cake?"

"The cake," she said. "And the sex. The cake wouldn't taste nearly as good without the sex. Although, the sex might have been even better had I known there was cake at the end." She bumped against his shoulder then gave him a quick kiss. "Is Tally put to bed?"

Logan nodded and took another bite of the cake. "If it's all right with you, I think we should take a couple days in Adelaide. Tally could use the break and so could we."

"I don't need to be anywhere," she said. "I'm enjoying this trip."

"We've got a long stretch of outback to get through tomorrow." He reached out and took her hand, then pressed a kiss to the spot below her wrist. "I'm glad you're going to be there when I have to give her up. It will make it a lot easier."

"You are going to miss her," she said softly.

Logan nodded. "Yeah. I've raised her, I've seen her almost every day in the last three years. She has this personality and it's like we know each other so well."

Sunny set the box down beside her and wrapped her arms around his neck, giving him a fierce hug. "I understand," she murmured. "Really, I do."

"I know," he said. And she did. She was maybe

the only person who truly would know how hard it was for him to give Tally away. Logan flopped back onto the bed and Sunny curled up beside him, throwing her leg over his hips.

They lay quietly, Logan listening to the rhythm of his own breathing. He was starting to come to grips with losing Tally. But at the same time, he was wondering how he'd ever let Sunny go.

Before they slept, he pulled her into his arms and made love to her once more, this time slowly, savoring every single moment between them. It was all right to dream about the life he wanted someday. But it wasn't very practical to wish for things that he couldn't possibly possess.

Sunny was one of those impossible dreams. Though he could see a future in his mind's eye, he didn't really want to believe it could happen for him. It was best to keep his hopes and dreams based in reality and not pure fantasy.

4

"Good morning, darling. Did you have a good night?"

Sunny ran her hand over the filly's nose, and the horse nodded her head. Tally had such a sweet disposition that Sunny had already fallen in love with her. Though she felt a bit guilty about her feelings, she knew Padma would understand. There was enough room in her heart for two favorite horses.

"We girls have to stick together," she murmured.

Her father had tried for years to get her to ride a gelding, but Sunny had stubbornly insisted that her mare could jump just as well as any male—or formerly male—mount. It wasn't accepted wisdom in the equestrian world. Very few show jumpers rode mares. But she felt a duty to at least promote the idea that female horses were good for more than just breeding.

She clipped a lead onto Tally's halter and slowly led her down the ramp. The horse seemed grateful to be out of the confines of her traveling coach and pranced along beside her. Sunny attached her to the secure line and Tally bent down and began to nibble at the damp morning grass.

The sun was just above the horizon. Glancing over her shoulder, Sunny wondered how much time she'd have before Logan woke up. They had a long drive ahead of them, most of it a straight line through the desolate outback, but she found herself looking forward to the time on the road. She and Logan made good traveling companions.

She'd never thought much about the kind of man she wanted in her life. She'd pretty much enjoyed whatever sort wandered through. But spending time with Logan, Sunny realized there were certain qualities she needed to find in a long-term prospect.

A tiny smile curved her lips and she shook her head. She'd never been the kind of girl who thought about forever, especially when it came to men. But now, she realized she'd just never met a man who was so perfectly suited to her personality as Logan was.

He had a calming effect on her, a way of making her slow down and think before she reacted. And he didn't tell her what she wanted to hear—he told her the truth. If she was acting like a brat, he called her a brat. He wouldn't allow her to goad him into an argument, thus making it impossible to have the tempestuous type of relationship that she'd always sought in the past.

It was strange how her whole attitude had changed since she'd met him. After London, she was like a ship without a rudder, just circling aimlessly with no destination in mind. But now, she felt focused, completely aware of who she was and what she was doing. And she wanted to ride again.

Not just ride, she thought. Really train. Get her mind and her body into the right place to win. Immerse herself in the sport. She was never more comfortable than when she was in the saddle. But now, she realized she could be comfortable off the horse as well—with Logan.

She leaned against the wall of the trailer and closed her eyes. Though she was twenty-six years old, Sunny had never really felt like a woman. And now she did. Now she knew what she wanted from her life, and it wasn't just cute boys and expensive things. She wanted a man who fed her soul, who made her laugh. A man who expected her to be a better person.

She drew a deep breath and shook her head. Though life on the road seemed to pass at a slow pace, Sunny felt as if she were on board a runaway train. Everything about her was changing inside and she couldn't keep up. The problem was she didn't want to keep up. She just wanted to let it all happen.

Opening her eyes, Sunny glanced around the interior of the trailer. Her gaze fell on the wire racks in the front that held feed and straw. Above that, she'd noticed an old saddle and bridle, and she grabbed them both, then searched for a saddle pad.

The pad was buried under a moldy duffel bag. She shook the straw off it, then walked out of the trailer into the new morning. "Look what I found," she said, calling to the filly.

Tally perked her head up and slowly walked toward her. When Sunny reached her side, she set the saddle down and examined it carefully. The leather was dry and cracked and the fittings tarnished, but the cinch was still strong.

"You wanna go for a ride?" she asked. She smoothed the pad over the filly's back then lifted the English saddle over the pad. "We're going to have some fun, you and I."

The bridle was in better condition than the saddle, but it needed adjustments before it fit the filly properly. Sunny worked at the buckles and snaps, and when she was satisfied, she unclipped Tally from the rope line and jumped up into the saddle.

Gathering the reins between her fingers, she softly clucked her tongue and touched her heels to the horse's flanks. Tally immediately sprang into action with a quick walk.

Sunny had a very precise warm-up and she took her new mount through the paces, learning to read the horse's reactions and adjusting her commands along the way. When they were both warmed up, she nudged the horse into a slow gallop and made a big circle around the campground lawn.

Tally was grateful for the freedom, and Sunny wished that she had an open field or a dirt track so she could give the filly her head and let her fly.

When they'd made two circles around the grassy area, she let the reins go slack, and Tally continued in the wide arc. Sunny let her hands drop to her side, then closed her eyes and tipped her head back.

The connection between them was so perfect. They moved together, like one being. Sunny held her arms out and smiled. She was a horse, running through an open field, the sun growing warm on her back, the air crisp in her nose, her mane flying out behind her.

She heard a whistle and felt the horse shift beneath her. Opening her eyes, she saw Logan standing in the doorway of the campervan. He watched her with a smile on his face and he waved to her.

She grabbed the reins and steered Tally toward the campervan, drawing her to a stop in front of Logan. "She's wonderful."

"You look wonderful on her," he said.

She bent over the horse's neck and hugged her. "Then sell her to me. I promise, I'll take good care of her."

Sunny saw the change in his expression, the

shadow of regret that colored his reaction. "I can't," he said. "The deal is made. There's nothing I can do."

"I'll make you a better deal," she said. She could see how much Logan loved the filly. It just didn't seem fair that he had been forced to sell her, especially to someone he didn't know.

"I bet you will."

She met his gaze, staring at him with a stubborn tilt to her head. "I'm not going to give up. By the time we get to Perth, she's going to be mine. You won't be able to say no." With that, Sunny pulled the horse around and continued her circle of the lawn. "Can she jump?" she called.

"I never tried," he said.

"Go inside and get a blanket, the white one."

He did as she asked and she explained how to lay it out on the ground in a long, narrow rectangle.

"What are you going to do?"

"See if she'll jump over it."

"She'll just run over it," he said with a smile.

"Maybe, maybe not. Go grab a few of the cushions and put them on top of the blanket." When the impromptu jump was constructed, Sunny brought the horse to a slow gallop again and, carefully controlling her speed, turned her toward the jump.

To her surprise, the filly didn't rush or balk. She neatly leaped over the obstacle as if she'd been doing it her entire life. Sunny glanced over at Logan. "See."

"That was beautiful."

"She wants to jump. She's meant to jump."

"I'm going to walk over to the restaurant and get us some breakfast." He turned to walk back inside.

"I'm not going to give up," she called after him.

Sunny continued to ride until Logan left, then cooled the filly down and got her fed. The ride had left her sweaty, so she grabbed a towel and her cotton dress and headed for the showers.

It was going to be a long day on the road, and it felt good to work off a little excess energy before heading out. She ran her fingers through her hair then lathered it up with the shampoo that Logan had bought her.

When they got to Adelaide, they'd need to pick up the package that Lily had sent her. After that, she and Logan would be free to enjoy themselves, with an unlimited budget available for hotel rooms and decent meals. But Sunny knew she'd need to proceed carefully. Logan had his pride and he could be stubborn. He wasn't going to appreciate her throwing her wealth around as if she thought nothing of it.

She stepped out of the shower and wrapped the towel around her wet hair, then pulled the dress over her damp skin. The thin fabric clung to her curves but she didn't care. After brushing her teeth, she gathered her riding clothes and slipped into her shoes.

The few campers in the campground were still asleep as she headed back to the campervan. Tally walked up to her and nudged her hand, looking for a treat, but she gave the filly a pat on the nose and continued on.

The breakfast bags were sitting on the table when she stepped inside. But Logan was nowhere to be found. She opened a carton and grabbed a piece of bacon, nibbling on it as she went back to the door. She saw him coming across the lawn, his hair damp from the showers. He was bare chested, a towel draped around his neck.

She felt a warm rush of desire at the sight of him. He was such a beautiful man, long limbed and slender hipped, his broad chest burnished by the sun. He stopped to rub Tally's nose, then continued toward her.

"I am ready to eat," he announced.

"Me, too," she said.

As he stepped into the campervan, he grabbed her waist and pulled her into a long, deep, electrifying kiss. Sunny moaned as she dropped her things on the floor and wrapped her arms around his neck. Logan gently tugged the towel from her hair and tossed it aside. His fingers tangled in the damp strands and he molded her mouth to his.

When he finally drew away, she was breathless, her heart beating at a frantic rate. Logan kissed the tip of her nose and then dropped one more kiss on her lips. "I think we better eat our breakfast and get on the road."

She smoothed her palm down his chest and then lower, to the front of his jeans. She could feel the stiff ridge beneath the denim. "What are we going to do with this?" she asked.

"I'm sure that will go away on its own. Don't worry. There are more where that came from."

Sunny giggled then kissed him again. "Good. I'll be counting on that."

As Sunny finished unpacking the breakfast and spread it on the table, he wrapped his arms around her waist and rested his chin on her shoulder. This was what it was between them, these easy, sweet mornings followed by wild, passionate nights. She could survive forever living a life like this, Sunny mused. Anywhere, as long as Logan was with her.

She drew a deep breath and closed her eyes for a moment. It seemed like a dream. But then, sometimes dreams did come true.

THEY'D SPENT ALMOST the entire day driving southwest on the narrow sealed road, a straight and seemingly endless line through the outback.

The towns were few and far between, sometimes more than a hundred kilometers between anything remotely civilized. Logan couldn't imagine what the endless stretch would have been like without Sunny's company. But between the music and the sound of her voice, the drive was bearable. No, it was actually enjoyable.

She made everything so much more fun. And he hadn't had this much fun in his life for a long time. He hadn't really thought it was important to laugh and be silly. From the time he was a child, he'd taken a serious approach to life. His father had moved from job to job, mostly finding work on sheep stations or cattle ranches in desolate areas of the outback.

All of this emptiness brought back old memories, those days that they'd travel, looking for work, wondering where the next meal would come from. His younger brother had suffered most. They'd both overheard the conversations, his father's angry outbursts, his mother's sobbing pleas. But Sam hadn't been able to deal with the fear and uncertainty as Logan had.

"New game," Sunny said, reaching over to touch his arm.

"No more memory games," he said. "You beat me every time."

"No. This is called What Were You Thinking?"

"Are we going to talk about selling Tally again?"

"No, I want to know what you were just thinking. And you have to answer me honestly. Complete and total honesty."

Logan shook his head. He'd told her stories about his childhood and his family, but they'd been shined up and all the sad and pathetic details had been omitted. He shouldn't have lied, but he'd never thought there'd be a time he'd want to tell the truth.

"I was just thinking about when me and my family would travel through the outback. Just recalling all those old feelings I had."

"What kind of feelings?"

He paused, considering how to explain to her. "Dread," he finally said. "Fear. Frustration." He glanced over at her. Her expression had changed from lighthearted curiosity to concern. "It just wasn't a good time in my life."

"Tell me," she said softly. "I really want to know."

"My dad never had a good job. We moved from place to place while he looked for work, usually on sheep stations or cattle ranches. Sometimes they had a house for us. Usually it was more like a shack. And sometimes we lived in a tent." He shook his head. "School was always a spotty thing. If we lived near a town, my little brother and I would go, usually dressed in the same clothes every day. But if we were out in the bush, my mom would teach us. I always liked that."

"How did you learn about horses?"

"I worked a horse farm during my summers off from high school. I got a scholarship to a private boys' school, but I couldn't stay there in the summer and my folks didn't need me around, so I worked. Learned everything I could about horses. Then I worked my way through university and took a job at a bank and started saving to buy my own place." He chuckled softly. "And here I am with you."

"What is your brother doing now?"

Logan drew a deep breath. It was still difficult to talk about. "He died when I was at university. He got mixed up with drugs and he died. He was never really into school, so he stayed with my parents until he was sixteen and then took off on his own. I tried to help him out, but he was pretty mad at me for leaving him."

She reached out and smoothed her hand over his cheek. "I'm so sorry," she murmured.

Logan grabbed her fingers and placed a kiss in the middle of her palm. It felt good to tell her, as if a weight had been lifted from him. "Now you have to tell me one of your sad stories. If you have any."

"Oh, I have plenty," she said. "But I will tell you one. I think if I had to pick one thing that defined my life, it would be the time that I realized my mother and father didn't have a marriage."

"How did that happen?"

"My parents were fighting, but this time it was really big. My mother had shut herself in her room and she wasn't coming out and I was supposed to go get new riding boots for a competition, so my father took me to his office and we were supposed to be there for just a few minutes so he could make a phone call. But then, this woman showed up and they were arguing and whispering and she was touching him and trying to kiss him and I knew something was up. I was nine years old and I could feel it."

She sighed. "They sent me out of the office and

they stayed in there a long, long time. And when the woman came out, she smiled at me, but it wasn't a nice smile. I could tell she hated me."

"I'm sorry," he said.

"For what?"

"That you had to go through that."

Sunny shrugged. "I guess, in the end, it was better to know. It explained a lot of what was going on in our house. Why my mother was so angry and why my father paid more attention to my riding career than he did to her." She forced a smile. "It did kind of screw me up as far as men went. I guess you could say I have trust issues."

"Do you trust me?" he asked.

A smile broke across her face and she nodded. "I do. That's the really strange thing. The minute I met you, I just felt it. That's why I slept with you that night. Because I knew I could trust you. It's why I didn't want you to take me back home."

"We make quite a pair," he said.

Sunny nodded. "Yes, we do."

As they got nearer and nearer to the coast, the landscape gradually changed. Barren land gave way to ranches, then farms; the towns came in closer succession, and the endless horizon was broken by the dark outline of Mount Remarkable in the distance.

Ed had given Logan the name of a horse breeder with a farm about forty-five minutes outside of Adelaide, and he was glad to see a tiptop operation as they rolled up the driveway. The stable manager met them outside the barn and was happy to board and exercise Tally for the next two nights.

When Logan offered to pay him, he refused, saying there might come a day when Logan could be of assistance to him. Logan suspected that it was Ed who would be of assistance and not a second-rate horse breeder from the middle of nowhere.

While Logan got Tally settled in a stall and brought out her feed and grooming supplies, Sunny wandered around the stables, looking at the horses. He saw her chatting with one of the grooms and before long, she had a small group gathered around her.

She glanced over at him and he sent her a quizzical look, wondering if she needed to be rescued. A small shrug told him that for the moment, she was fine, so he continued his work.

Logan smiled to himself as he rubbed Tally's nose. He and Sunny had spent so much time together over the past few days that they were now able to communicate without even talking. But then, that shouldn't surprise him.

He leaned back against the plank wall and remembered their encounter last night. They hadn't needed words then, either. A shiver ran through him and he sucked in a sharp breath. Logan knew he ought to just be happy with what he had at the moment—a beautiful, sexy woman in his bed. But it was human nature to want more.

He'd had plenty of time to work it all out in his head, but no matter which way he turned it, he couldn't see anything more than an occasional weekend together. Once she got back to riding again, she'd be busy. And his ranch was an eight-hour drive from her parents' place.

A groan rumbled in his chest and he ran his hands through his hair. Why even think about this now? He should just enjoy his good fortune while he had it. Who knew when he might get so lucky again?

"Are you all right?"

He glanced up to see Sunny standing at the stall door. Strange how just looking at her made him feel better. "Yeah, I'm good."

"Can I help you with anything?"

Logan shook his head. "Naw, you just stand there looking pretty."

"I called Lily and she told me that my package is waiting at my father's Adelaide office."

"What does your father do?"

"He's into energy," she said. "Oil, petrol, electricity. I really don't know all the details."

"My power bill is overdue," Logan joked. "You think he could help me out with that?"

"Next time I see him, I'll ask."

She stepped inside the stall and wrapped her arms around his neck, then gave him a kiss, her tongue teasing at his until he was forced to drop the pitchfork and wrap his hands around her waist.

"I'm never going to be finished if you keep interrupting me," he murmured, pressing his lips to her neck.

"Stop complaining," she replied.

"Oh, I'm not complaining. I'm just looking forward to the rest of the night."

BY THE TIME SUNNY and Logan got to Adelaide, it was nearly seven o'clock. Sunny had thought about stopping at her father's office the next morning, but when she called, she was surprised that the receptionist was still waiting for her arrival.

Logan stayed in the campervan while she went inside the glass-and-steel building in the downtown business district. A pretty girl sat behind a wide desk, the Grant Energies logo on a wall behind her.

"Are you Sunny?"

Sunny smiled and nodded. "I'm so sorry to make you wait."

"Oh, no worries. I was happy to do it." She picked up a large box and set it on the counter. "Your father's assistant took the liberty of preparing our beach villa and you're welcome to stay there while you're in the area. It's just fifteen minutes from here." She handed Sunny another envelope. "It's a lovely place on the water."

She stared down at the envelope. Her father had a beach villa? "Thank you," Sunny murmured. "And thank my father's assistant. I'll be sure to mention her kindness. And yours."

The receptionist smiled. "There's a map in the envelope. And the combination for the lockbox with the key. Have a lovely time."

"We will," she said.

A man suddenly appeared, picked up the box and nodded at her. Sunny glanced back and forth between the receptionist and him. "This is Darrell. He'll help you with your box."

Sunny turned and walked to the door, smiling to herself. She knew her father was a very successful businessman. When they traveled to equestrian events or went on holiday, the accommodations were always first-rate. But she never knew that he employed so many people just to take care of the details of his life. Too bad he couldn't find someone to bring her mother back from Paris.

Sunny held the door open for Darrell, and when they reached the street, Logan was standing next to the campervan. Darrell took in the battered state of their vehicle and gave her an odd look.

"I can take that," Logan offered.

"Where do you want it?" Darrell asked.

He quickly opened the side door to the campervan and Darrell set it inside. Then Darrell turned to Sunny and nodded. "You have a fine evening, Miss Grant. Drive safely."

"Thank you," Sunny said.

Logan stepped to her side as she watched Darrell walk back inside. "Should we have tipped him?"

She shook her head. "No, he works for my father. I'm sure he's well paid." She turned to him. "We have to talk."

"What?"

She saw concern cross his features and she reached out and took his hand. "You know how I said we could rent a room tonight and maybe sleep in a real bed. And have a real shower?"

He nodded. "We don't have to do that. There are plenty of nice campgrounds in—"

"I know a place where we can stay for free," she said. "My father's assistant set it up."

"I'm all for that," Logan said. "No need to spend money when we don't have to."

"All right, then. Let's go."

The got back into the campervan and Sunny pulled the map out of the envelope. Her father's assistant had drawn a line from the office to the Henley Beach villa.

"Where are we going?"

"Just turn left and then forward until the next signal."

They found the beach villa without any trouble, and when Sunny hopped out of the campervan, she smiled. Though the villa blocked the view of the water, she could smell the sea in the air and could hear the waves over the traffic on the street.

She grabbed Logan's hand and pulled him along to the front door. As promised, there was a lockbox. She punched in the code and it opened, revealing a set of keys. Sunny unlocked the door and they walked inside.

The interior was airy and spacious. Through a wide wall of windows on the beach side of the villa, Sunny could see the sunset, a blaze of orange and pink.

Logan slowly walked over to the windows and stared out. "Holy shit," he murmured.

She ran over to him and threw her arms around his neck. "Is it all right? Can we stay? It is free."

He slipped his arms around her waist and pulled her close. "Yeah, I think we can stay. Hell, maybe we should just move in."

She unlocked the door to the terrace and walked outside. A narrow path through the scrub led to a beautiful white-sand beach. She looked up and down the beach and in the distance saw a high jetty jutting out into the water. This was the perfect spot to relax for the next few days. "Thank you, Daddy," she shouted.

She turned around and walked back inside to find Logan standing in the kitchen, the refrigerator door held open. "You should see what's inside here," he said. He pulled out a bottle of champagne and held it up. "Do they think we're on our honeymoon?"

"They're just making us comfortable."

"Well, I would have been happy with a beer and some crisps."

"So what should we do? There's a pier not far from here. Maybe we could walk down and see what's happening." She paused. "Or we could check out the bed. See if it's comfortable." Sunny slowly approached him, unbuttoning the front of her dress. "Or we could always take a shower."

He chuckled softly. "Why don't I go get that big box of yours and we'll change and take a walk. I need to stretch my legs before you put me through my paces in the bedroom."

"Giddy up," she said with a teasing glint in her eye.

They hurried outside to the campervan and gathered up all their things, then carried them inside. Sunny tore open the box and was thrilled to find that Lily had packed some of her favorite things.

She dumped everything out on the bed then hung the clothes up in the closet. She slipped out of her dress and put on her hot-pink bikini, pulling a comfortable cotton dress over the top. She found a pair of thongs in the bottom of the box and slipped them on her bare feet, then went to find Logan.

He was sitting on the terrace, his long legs stretched out in front of him, a beer in his hand. His sunglasses shielded his eyes against the sunset, and when she stepped outside, he held out his hand.

Sunny placed her fingers in his and he pulled

her hand to his lips. "It's a whole different world," he said.

She knew how he must feel, especially after all the things he had told her about his family. To him, money meant comfort and security. But what he didn't understand was that sometimes all the money in the world couldn't make a person feel as safe as she did with him.

Sunny wanted to find the words to tell him that, to tell him how wonderful he was and how perfect he made her feel and how she didn't think of their differences when they were together. But she'd never completely understand what he'd gone through.

"It's a perfect summer night," she said. "Let's enjoy ourselves while we're here."

"I can do that," he said.

They walked down to the water and dipped their bare feet in, letting the waves wash up as they stared out over the Indian Ocean at the setting sun. From a distance, Sunny could hear music, and they picked up their shoes and started down the beach.

Logan draped his arm around her shoulders as they walked, and they chatted about simple things, riding and horses, Sunny's competitions and Logan's ranch. They never seemed to run out of topics. One question always led to another. And when there was silence between them, it was because they just wanted to enjoy being together and not because they didn't have anything to say.

When they reached the jetty, they walked up toward the street and found a huge square. A band played on one end and people had gathered with food and drinks, to watch. Logan grabbed them each a beer from the bar and they found a place to sit.

As they watched the band, Logan seemed to lose himself in his thoughts. When he finished his beer, he got another. Sunny watched him, worried that she'd done or said something wrong.

When the band took a break, they walked out to the end of the jetty. He leaned over the rail, resting his arms as he stared out at the sea. Slipping her arms around his, she rested her head on his shoulder. "If this is too much, we can find somewhere else to stay."

"No, this isn't too much," he said. "It's just… perfect. Really, it is."

"It's not who I am," Sunny said. "Maybe it used to be, but not anymore. It's not important."

"That's easy to say. Especially when you have everything you could possibly want."

"I don't," she said. "I have nothing that I really want."

He laughed and glanced over at her. "I find that hard to believe."

"It's true."

"What do you want that you don't have?"

"A life of my own. A future. Someone who'll love

me forever. I want to get up in the morning and have something important to do."

"You have your riding."

"Is that really important?" she asked. "If I stop riding tomorrow, no one would care. No one would miss me. I want to be an important part of someone else's life. I want someone to need me and to miss me if I'm not there."

"And I want to wake up someday and not have to worry about where the next dollar is going to come from," he said. "I want to stop worrying about what I might lose and just enjoy what I have."

She gave his arm a squeeze, wishing she could just wipe away the doubts in his mind. They were from two different worlds, but some strange twist of fate had put them together, and Sunny sensed that, sooner or later, the reason would be revealed.

She had always believed in destiny, in the idea that there were forces at work in her life that would determine her future. But she was coming to understand that she could have a hand in her fate, that she could even control it if she wanted.

What would it take to become a permanent part of Logan's world? How would she convince him to be part of hers? Were they so different that it would be impossible to find a place where they could exist together?

"You are the most wonderful man I've ever known," she said. "You're kind and patient and funny and romantic, and all of those things mean so much more than what's in your bank account."

"Pretty words," he murmured.

"Just because they're pretty doesn't mean they're not true." She pulled him away from the railing. "Come on. Let's go back."

He reluctantly straightened, then took her hand. "I'm hungry."

"I'll make you something," Sunny said.

"You can cook?"

"Yes, I can cook. I used to spend a lot of time hanging out with the help."

"Well, this should be interesting," he said with a grin. "I never would have guessed you could cook."

"There's a lot you don't know about me," she said.

Logan nodded. "I'm beginning to realize that."

5

LOGAN STOOD ON THE TERRACE, staring out at the black horizon, the sound of the waves lulling him into a sense of comfort.

He and Sunny had a late dinner and then decided to curl up on the sofa and watch a movie. But she'd fallen asleep after just ten minutes. He glanced over his shoulder and smiled.

He liked the way she looked when she slept. It was a different, more relaxed Sunny. When she was awake, she was always bubbling with energy. Even in their quiet moments, he could sense her mind running at high speed. But when she slept, she was still, her body relaxed and her mind at peace.

She was so different from the woman he'd first thought she was. When she had climbed up on that fence, dressed in nothing but her T-shirt and pink bikini bottoms, his first impression had not been all good. She'd seemed prickly and difficult, like a girl with a chip on her shoulder. But then she'd smiled and everything changed.

He knew the first time he looked into her eyes that all that bravado was hiding some very deep hurt. He'd always thought that money was the only thing that could buy happiness, but now he knew the truth. Sunny had all the advantages anyone could want, yet she didn't have what she really needed— unconditional love.

Logan cursed beneath his breath. Was he prepared to give that to her? The longer they spent together, the more he found himself imagining a life with Sunny. Part of that fantasy required him forgetting about the objections her family might have, and ignoring the money issue and the fact that she probably wouldn't want to live in the outback. But once he factored out all those things, it did make a lovely little dream.

"Jaysus," he muttered. There was delusion and then there was just outright batty. If he were thinking with his head, instead of his libido, he'd send her home tomorrow. Or leave her to her daddy's luxury apartment while he drove off into the distance.

There were plenty of other women in the world who'd find life on a dusty old horse ranch to be an adventure or a challenge. He just couldn't see Sunny among that group.

"Let her go," he murmured to himself. "Make a clean break and walk away."

It made perfect sense. He wasn't at a point in his life when he could afford to fall in love. Life was hard enough looking after himself and the ranch. He didn't need another responsibility. So he'd spend the next few days with Sunny, enjoying her company, and then, in the middle of the night, he'd leave.

She'd understand, Logan rationalized. She knew as well as he did that any future between them was doomed. So why not just enjoy their attraction for a bit longer and call an end to it, sensibly, without any regrets?

Or why not just leave now? Sunny was safe here. She had a place to stay until she went back home. It would be simple enough for her to get a flight to Brisbane. Now would be the best time, he told himself.

But was it the coward's way out? Would he leave to make things easier for her—or for him? Falling in love with Sunny was the last thing in the world he wanted to do. It would only cause more complications in a relationship that was complicated already.

"Just go," he murmured. Turning away from the railing, he walked back into the villa. Sunny didn't stir as he passed on his way to the bedroom. Logan silently began to gather his things, stowing them in his rucksack.

When he was finished, he stood beside the empty

bed, considering what he was about to do. There'd be no going back. Any future that he might have dreamed about with Sunny would evaporate.

Gathering his resolve, Logan walked back through the villa and paused as he passed the sofa. Scanning Sunny's profile, he tried to commit the last details to memory. It would be a long time before he forgot her—and the time they spent together.

He turned and walked to the door, then opened it slowly. She'd be fine. This was all going to come to an end anyway. Better sooner than later.

The night air was chilly as Logan walked out to the campervan. He opened the door and sat down behind the wheel, tossing his rucksack onto the passenger seat. But when he pulled his keys out of his pocket, he couldn't bring himself to go any further.

His gaze fell on the volume of Shakespeare sitting on the console between the seats. They were in the middle of *As You Like It,* a play made much better by Sunny's narration. He picked the book up and opened it, then pulled out a bubblegum wrapper she was using as a bookmark. She'd bought a handful of bubblegum a few days ago and they'd spent a hundred-kilometer stretch outside of Bourke in a bubble-blowing contest.

As he looked around the campervan, there were reminders of her everywhere. Cursing softly, he flipped on the overhead light and moved into the back, picking up Sunny's things along the way. She'd made herself at home, that much was clear.

Logan stopped short and tossed the items onto the sofa. This was crazy. Just because he rid himself of her things it wouldn't stop the memories from coming. He got back behind the wheel and reached for the ignition. But a knock on the window startled him.

He glanced to his left and saw Sunny standing outside, wrapped in a blanket, her hair tumbled down around her face. Logan rolled down the window.

"What are you doing out here?" she asked. "I woke up and I couldn't find you."

He scrambled for an answer. He couldn't tell her the truth—it would only hurt her. "I—I thought I left a light on and I just wanted to check to see if it drained the battery." He turned the ignition and the campervan started. "It's all right. Go inside. I'm just going to let it run for a while. I'll be in in a few minutes."

She gave him a puzzled look then nodded. "All right. But hurry up."

Logan watched as she walked back to the villa. Groaning, he bent his head over the steering wheel, resting it against his clasped hands. What the hell was he doing? It might very well be the noble thing to do, to break things off cleanly now. But the only one he was really protecting was himself.

Sunny was a big girl. She knew the pitfalls of love, probably better than he did. When things didn't work out in the end, she'd go on with her life. She'd find a nice guy, maybe settle into a good relationship and eventually get married.

He'd be the one left regretting what could have been, wondering if he'd had more to offer he might have convinced her there was a future between them. She was right here, standing in front of him, offering him fantasies that would last a lifetime and he was too afraid to reach out and grab them.

With another curse, Logan turned off the ignition and jumped out of the campervan. He wasn't going to be the one to end it. He would leave that up to her. And when it happened, he'd be grateful for the time they'd had and go on with his life.

When he got back inside, he dropped his rucksack on the floor beside the sofa and walked into the bedroom. Sunny was already in bed, curled up beneath a down duvet. He stripped off his clothes and crawled between the crisp bed linens, snuggling up against her naked body.

A soft sigh slipped from her lips, and she reached back and tangled her fingers in his hair, pulling him closer. Logan pressed a kiss to the curve of her neck, his lips finding her pulse point.

She gently guided him inside her, and for a long time they didn't move. He thought that she might have fallen asleep, but when he smoothed his palm down her belly to the juncture between her legs, she moaned softly. Logan touched her, gently rubbing his fingers over the core of her desire.

He felt her grow damp around him, and then a delicious heat that he found irresistible. Every instinct told him to move, but he stayed still, enjoying the changes in Sunny's body as she came closer and closer to her release.

When it finally came, it was quiet yet incredibly powerful. He felt every spasm of her body as he held her close. She melted against him, boneless and relaxed. Then, in two quick thrusts, he was there himself, tumbling over the edge and losing control deep inside her.

They didn't speak, both of them completely sated. Logan listened as her breathing grew slow and deep and before long, he knew she was asleep again.

"What the hell am I going to do about you, Sunny Grant?" he whispered. It was so easy to say he wouldn't fall for her, but harder to admit that he already was—deeply and madly in love with Sunny.

SUNNY RAKED HER HANDS through her hair as she sat up in bed. She glanced over at the clock and saw it was nearly nine. She wasn't even sure when they'd finally gotten to sleep last night, but she'd slept so soundly she felt refreshed.

Glancing over at Logan, Sunny could tell he was still a few hours from getting up. In normal life, between the two of them, he was the early riser, but since they'd been spending their nights in carnal pursuits, he usually slept until she woke him up.

Sunny carefully crawled out of bed and searched the floor for something to wear. She pulled a T-shirt from her bag and tugged it over her head, then headed to the kitchen. But as she passed the sofa, she noticed Logan's rucksack sitting on the floor.

She picked it up, wondering why he'd left it where he had. Curious, Sunny opened it up and rummaged through his belongings, a strange realization setting in. Everything was inside. His clothes, his shaving kit, everything that he'd—

Sucking in a sharp breath, Sunny dropped the rucksack on the floor. It all made sense now. Last night. The campervan. He was going to leave. If she hadn't found him gone and searched him out, she'd be alone right now.

Sunny wasn't sure how to feel. Should she be hurt or angry? Should she confront him and get to the truth of the matter? What other explanation could there be? Slowly she sat down on the end of the sofa, then buried her face in her hands.

Maybe she'd just been fooling herself. They'd been getting along so well, enjoying their trip. But she had to wonder if the attraction was all one-sided. Yes, they had a fantastic sexual relationship, but the men she'd known had always been able to separate affection from sexual desire.

Was that all it was? Was he afraid that her feelings

were deeper than what he was prepared to handle? Sunny thought back over the past few days, wondering if she had said or done something to scare him off. God, how did she always manage to pick men who were emotionally unavailable?

So what was she supposed to do now? Was this just a momentary crisis or did he still have plans to desert her along the way? She'd never asked for any type of commitment from him, so why was he so afraid that he wanted to leave her? She leaned back into the suede sofa and stared up at the ceiling.

Maybe he was worried she'd be the one to leave. Could she really blame him? He saw her life as perfect and only because she'd never had to worry about money. But he refused to see that her happiness didn't come from financial security, it came from feeling loved and wanted.

Sunny pushed to her feet and walked to the kitchen. She'd just pretend she never saw it. That was the only thing she could do. That…and wait. She pulled open the refrigerator door and peered inside. Breakfast. That would take her mind off the rucksack sitting beside the sofa.

Her father's assistant had provided them with a wide variety of food for any meal they might want to prepare. Sunny pulled out a grapefruit, a carton of eggs, a package of bacon and some English muffins. She even found a jug of fresh orange juice.

A tin of coffee came next, and Sunny scooped

enough into a filter to make a strong brew. She filled the coffeemaker and flipped it on, then started the rest of the preparations.

They had a whole day here in Adelaide and until this morning, she'd been looking forward to it. Tomorrow, they'd be back on the road, driving the last few days to Perth. She couldn't spend that whole time wondering what he was thinking and feeling. And she certainly couldn't sleep with him, knowing what she knew.

"Oh, that will be easy," she muttered as she put the bacon in the microwave. She'd never been able to hold her tongue. Usually, when she was upset by something, she couldn't stop talking about it. And Sunny had always been able to hold a grudge much longer than anyone she knew.

She dumped the eggs into a sauté pan and stirred them. It would probably be best if she just let it go. Maybe her suspicions were wrong. Maybe he was just keeping his things tidy, or maybe he expected a fire or an earthquake or—

For the next five minutes, she concentrated on the breakfast preparations. When everything was ready, she set it all on a tray and carried it into the bedroom. Logan was still in exactly the same position he'd been in when she'd left. She sank down on the bed and he stirred.

"Are you awake?" Sunny asked.

"Mmm. Is that bacon I smell?"

"I made breakfast."

He slowly rolled over to face her, then sat up, bracing himself on his outstretched arm. Raking his fingers through his tousled hair, he sent her a sleepy smile. "You made this?"

"Yeah. I thought it would be easier than going out." She pointed to the tray. "There's coffee, too. I forgot that."

She moved to get off the bed, but he caught her hand and pulled her close. "Good morning," he murmured, brushing a kiss across her lips.

"Morning," she said, her gaze meeting his.

Sunny quickly crawled off the bed. "I'll just get the coffee." She hurried to the kitchen and poured mugs for them both, adding sugar and cream to hers and just sugar to Logan's. She knew how he took his coffee. That was more than she'd ever bothered to learn about any of her other lovers. "What does that even mean?" she murmured.

As she walked back to the room, she grabbed the leather portfolio sitting on the coffee table and tucked it under her arm. The contents would provide something to talk about while Logan ate breakfast.

Sunny handed him the coffee, then took her place on the other side of the bed. "There's all sorts of information in here," she said, patting the front of the portfolio. "Things for us to do today." She opened it up and flipped through the pamphlets. She no-

ticed a note printed on Grant Energies letterhead
and pulled it out.

"'Use of the car,'" she read. "We have a car?"

"We do?"

Sunny crawled off the bed and ran back to the
kitchen, then walked out the front door. She found
the keypad to the left of the garage door and punched
in the security code written on the paper. The garage door opened, revealing a Volkswagen convertible and a Range Rover. "Wow, Daddy, that's a nice
surprise."

After she'd closed the garage door, she wandered
back inside and headed for the bedroom. "We have a
car," she said as she strolled back to the bed. "Two,
actually. A cute little convertible and a Range Rover.
So, I guess we can go anywhere we want today. My
father is paying for the petrol."

"Where would you like to go?"

Sunny began to pick through their options. She
felt his gaze on her and drew a deep breath, trying to
maintain her composure. It took every ounce of her
resolve to keep from asking him about the packed
rucksack. But she'd promised herself that she'd let
it go—for now.

She bit her bottom lip, fighting back a flood of
emotion. How could he even think of doing that to
her? She'd been deserted by every single person she'd
ever trusted in her life. First her mother, then her

father. Then every lover she'd ever taken. Had she made a mistake in trusting him, too?

"Wineries," she said. "Just south of here. That might be fun."

"Are you going to have any breakfast?" he asked, holding out a toasted English muffin.

She shook her head. "No, I'm not hungry right now."

"Are you feeling all right?"

Sunny glanced over her shoulder. "I'm fine."

"You're not fine. You never turn down breakfast."

"All right. Put some jam on that muffin. I'll have that." Sunny continued leafing through the pamphlets. She pulled out another. "Here. Sunset penguin tour on Granite Island. I want to do that, too."

"Penguins. That would be kind of cool."

"Good," she said, getting up from the bed. "While you're finishing your breakfast, I'm going to take a shower."

"Would you like me to join you?" he asked teasingly.

"I think I'll be fine on my own. There's more coffee in the kitchen."

With that, she walked through the bedroom into the bathroom and shut the door. Turning, she leaned back against it and closed her eyes. She could have walked right past that rucksack without even noticing it. If she had, she'd probably be happily sharing her shower with Logan, not putting doors between them.

She crossed to the sink and stared at her reflection in the mirror. Why did it even make a difference? So what if he'd been planning to abandon her? He wasn't any different than any other man she'd known in her life. Sooner or later, the affair ended and they disappeared.

It was no big deal. She just wouldn't allow herself to love him.

THEY LEFT THE VILLA after breakfast, driving the Volkswagen convertible out of the city. The morning was warm and the sky filled with fluffy white clouds. And for Logan, it was wonderful to be free of the lumbering campervan.

They stopped at a couple of wineries and enjoyed a tasting at each, but by the time they were headed to the third winery, Sunny was feeling the effects of the wine and Logan was feeling the effects of her mood.

"Where are we headed next?" Logan asked.

"I have no idea," she said, grinning. "Just keep driving until we see a sign with grapes on it. We'll figure it out then."

The views along the way were spectacular. When they weren't driving parallel along the water and beautiful white-sand beaches, they were winding through pretty little inland towns or speeding through wide meadows and low-lying hills.

He reached over and slipped his hand through the

hair at Sunny's nape. "Are you sure we shouldn't just stop and get some lunch?"

"No, I'm having fun. I'm seeing the countryside. I never really got to do that when I traveled for riding events. I always thought it would be fun to just take off and spend an entire summer traveling around the country. Maybe I'll get myself a campervan and do that."

Logan chuckled. "Just avoid the wineries."

Sunny unfolded the map she'd brought along and pointed to a sign up ahead. "Turn right at this next crossroads. There's another winery about a kilometer down the road."

Logan did as she asked, turning his attention back to the drive. Sunny hadn't been herself since they'd gotten up that morning. She was usually so full of energy that he had to constantly engage her in witty conversation or mind-numbing sex. But she'd been lost in her own thoughts and he couldn't help but wonder what was going on in her head.

Maybe another glass of wine would finally loosen her up a little bit. He'd stopped drinking after the first two samples, but she'd been enthusiastic about anything they offered.

They drove up a winding road shaded with trees, and stopped at a low stone building. The carved sign across the front was decorated with grapevines. Carney Creek Winery.

Logan parked the car and got out, jogging around

to open Sunny's door. But she'd already done that for herself. She stumbled slightly and he grabbed her hand as they walked to the front entrance, but before he opened it, Logan pulled them to a stop.

"Wait," he murmured.

"What?"

"Is everything all right?"

She gave him an impatient look. "Why do you keep asking me that?"

"Because you're acting…odd. You've been quiet. You've been drinking wine like you don't want to stop. Like maybe you're angry at me for something."

"Can we just go?"

Logan grabbed the heavy wooden door and pulled it open. They walked into a spacious room with timbered beams and stained-glass windows. A few other couples were wandering around the displays and chatting softly as relaxing music filled the interior.

The next tour was due to start in a half hour, but they were shown into the tasting room, where a young woman stood behind a counter, pouring wine into large crystal goblets.

They started out with white wines, and Sunny chatted with the young woman, the enologist, and listened to her describe the qualities of each sample. Logan sat next to her for a time then decided to leave her to her mood.

He walked back out to the shop and found a table, then flipped through a magazine about wine. There were things he'd never understand about women. If she was angry at him, why not just tell him? Why torture him for an entire morning?

Sunny had always been so open and honest with him and, suddenly, she wasn't interested in talking. His questions were answered with a single word or with a shrug. There was a storm brewing and he could feel it. He just wasn't sure when it would strike or why he was the target.

After the tasting, Sunny bought several bottles of wine and then found him outside. "I bought lunch," she said with a giggle. "I think we need to go to one more winery. I'm becoming an expert on wine."

"You're also a little drunk," he said.

"We're on holiday. I'm allowed to have fun, aren't I?"

Her tone was defensive, as if she was looking for an argument. But Logan wasn't going to rise to the bait. Sunny wasn't one to keep her feelings to herself. Given time, she'd say what was on her mind. He loved that they were so honest with each other. But maybe that time was over. Once they starting having expectations, there was much more opportunity for hurt feelings. Why couldn't things remain simple, he mused. The last thing he wanted to do was fight with her.

They walked back to the car park and Sunny climbed in the car and pulled out the map. When Logan got behind the wheel, he paused before reaching for the key in the ignition. "Do you want to tell me what's wrong or do you need a little more wine before that happens? We can just do it here in the car park."

"You want to do it here?" she said with a laugh.

"I want to discuss why you're cheesed off. And don't tell me that it's nothing. I've been living with you for the past five days. I know when something is bothering you."

"All right," she said, throwing her arms out and nearly hitting him in the face. "Let's just do that. And let's start with your rucksack."

"My rucksack?"

"Yes. I found it this morning, completely packed with everything you own, sitting on the floor near the sofa. So, either you were preparing for some type of natural disaster or you were going to leave last night. And," she added, her finger punching at his chest, "I found you out in the campervan. Care to explain?"

Logan winced. He hadn't realized until that morning that he'd left the rucksack where he had. He'd just assumed she hadn't noticed. "I was going to leave, but I changed my mind."

"Why? Why would you do that to me? I thought we were friends." She shoved the car door open and started off down the driveway, a bottle of wine still clutched in her hand.

"Sunny, stop." He went after her, but she turned

and threw the bottle at him. Logan dodged it and it fell into the long grass at the side of the road.

"I thought I could trust you. Why would you do that?"

"I was… I was scared. That if we stayed together any longer I'd fall in love with you."

She opened her mouth to shout at him then snapped it shut. Wiping a tear from her cheek, Sunny shook her head. "Well, what's so bad about that? Am I unlovable?" Tears filled her eyes. "That's why no one wants to stick around. Everyone leaves me. Except my horses. And they only stay because they're locked in the stables at night. They'd probably run away, too."

With a groan, she sat down in the middle of the road, burying her face in her hands. Logan ran over to her and grabbed her arms, pulling her to her feet. "Stop it, now," he said. "There's no reason to cry."

"Don't tell me what to do. I hate when people tell me what to do."

All that wine on an empty stomach was making Sunny slightly irrational, but Logan was determined to smooth things over. "I'm sorry. I was stupid."

"You're a coward."

"Yes," Logan said, ready to agree with anything she said. "I am."

She looked up at him. "I'm not going to fall in love with you. Don't you know that? I—I just can't let that happen." Tipping her chin up, she met his gaze. "We're just friends. Friends with benefits. That's all."

"That sounds just grand to me," Logan said. He motioned to her. "Come on. If we're going to go see the damn penguins, we need to leave now."

"The penguin tour is at dusk," Sunny pointed out.

"By dusk, you'll probably be sound asleep. If we can't see the penguins this afternoon, we won't be seeing the penguins."

Logan walked back to the car and Sunny reluctantly followed. Well, at least he got a chance to see a side of Sunny that wasn't normally visible. He couldn't blame her for acting like a brat. He knew she had issues with her parents abandoning her and what had he almost done? The same thing.

He held the car door open for her and she got inside, a dark expression on her face. When he was settled in the driver's seat, he turned to her. "I'm sorry. I never, ever meant to hurt you. I just thought it would be easier if we didn't let it go on too long. I thought we might develop feelings that complicated things. I was wrong. Now that I know exactly how you feel, I think we'll be all right."

Sunny glanced over at him. Her defiant expression dissolved and she leaned over and pressed her face into his shoulder. Logan slipped his arm around her and pulled her close. "I'm sorry," she murmured. "Sometimes I can be a real bitch."

"No," he said. "You aren't. It was all my fault."

"Maybe we could see the penguins another time. I think I'd really like to go back to the villa and spend the day sleeping on the beach."

"I think that would be a wonderful idea. Maybe we could drink that other bottle of wine you bought?"

She drew back then laughed. "If I wasn't getting a bloody headache, I might agree."

Logan started the car and they drove away from the winery. They'd had their first major argument and, looking back, it hadn't gone too badly.

"The penguins can wait," she murmured. "We'll see them another time. We could make a holiday of it, maybe next summer."

Next summer, Logan mused. So there was going to be a next summer between them? And he'd spent so much time worrying about next week.

6

SUNNY STRETCHED OUT in the wide chaise, stifling a yawn. They'd come back to the villa to spend the afternoon on the beach. The weather was warm and the skies were clear and after so much wine, Sunny was relaxed and sleepy.

She shaded her eyes and watched as Logan stood knee-deep in the water. Since her temper tantrum earlier that morning, he'd been quiet, his thoughts occupied with matters that he wasn't interested in sharing with her.

It didn't surprise her how the argument started. She'd been simmering since early that morning and the wine just made it easier to say what she was thinking. But after her fears and insecurities had been laid bare, Sunny felt a bit guilty. After all, she and Logan had known each other less than a week.

It wasn't fair to have any expectations this early on, was it?

And yet, she felt closer to Logan than she had to any other man she'd known. He was solid and honest, and he didn't get lost in his own ego. And even though she insisted he was just a friend, Sunny knew that wasn't true. She also knew that hiding her true feelings was the only way to keep him around. And that was her primary goal—to keep Logan in her life until he realized she was more important to him than any other person in his life.

It wasn't difficult to imagine what stood between them. They existed in totally different worlds. Hers was comfortable and his was a constant struggle. But she wasn't going to apologize for something she had no control over. Her father's money didn't define her.

She hadn't made her father wealthy, he did that on his own. And it wasn't her money. She was almost as poor as a church mouse. Her total wealth amounted to the credit limit on her bank card, and she wasn't even sure what that was.

Why couldn't they just be two people who shared an overwhelming passion for each other? Why did they have to live in the real world, where wealth seemed so important?

Logan ran back across the beach and plopped down next to her on the chaise. He shook his wet head, cold droplets falling over her warm skin. Sunny screamed and tried to scoot out of the way, but he grabbed her and pulled her back. His lips met hers in a long, lazy kiss.

"I think that we should do this every year," she murmured, running her fingers through his hair.

"What?" Logan said. "Kiss on the beach?"

"Travel. Go somewhere interesting. You have to admit, we make a good pair. We've only had one fight in five days and that was due to your stupidity and my overconsumption of wine."

"That's true," he admitted.

"And we don't have to rent separate rooms, so that saves money."

"Also true."

"So, I thought I could plan the trip and you'll come with me. For a week or two. It will be fun. Sex and travel. Doesn't that sound nice? And you could get away for a week or two, couldn't you?"

"I could," he said. "Where would you want to go?"

"Fiji. I've always wanted to go to Fiji. New Zealand. Bali. Iceland. There are so many interesting places. My mother lives in Paris. Paris is meant for lovers. Where would you like to go?"

"I've always wanted to go to Ireland," he said.

"Right. Quinn. That's Irish."

He nodded. "I probably have some relatives there, although I don't know for sure."

"That's where we'll go first then," she said. "It's a date."

"We'll see," he murmured.

"But, you have to say yes. I don't want to go with anyone else."

He slipped his arms around her waist and pulled her close. "Sunny, I don't know what I'll be doing next month, never mind two or three months from now. I don't make plans more than a week or two in advance."

"So what then? How am I supposed to think about you in the future?"

He stared at her for a long moment. "I don't know. I don't know what you want or what you expect. I just know that I can't offer you what you need."

"You don't have any idea what I need," Sunny said, her anger bubbling up inside her. God, there were times when she just wanted to shake him. He was so careful, so predictable. Why couldn't he just loosen up a little and live?

"Let's not argue," he said.

"No, let's. We've been telling each other the truth for the past five days, why stop now?"

He glanced around, as if worried that someone might overhear. "I'm not going to argue with you here. I don't even know what this is about."

"Don't just dismiss me," she said.

"Sunny, I'm not dismissing you. You want to talk about holidays, fine. Go ahead, I'm listening."

"Now you're pacifying me."

"Jaysus, I'm glad you know what I'm doing, because I sure don't."

"Well, let me give you some time to figure it out," she muttered, getting to her feet.

"Sunny, you know this is the wine talking."

"No, I'm fine. I just need some space." Sunny threw her towel around her neck and walked back to the villa. She shouldn't be surprised. They couldn't possibly agree on everything. But she thought at least he'd be interested in making some plans for the future.

She knew there wasn't much chance they'd have a real relationship. He lived in the outback and she was a city girl. And there was the money thing that always seemed to get in the way. But she'd be satisfied with an occasional getaway in some exotic location. What could be more fun?

Logan Quinn had no imagination. After their trip was over, he'd drop her at home and just drive away. How long would it take him to forget her? A month, maybe two? Well, she never had any intention of remembering him anyway.

She cursed softly, trudging through the sand. But as she climbed the steps to the villa, she looked up to find a figure standing in the open doorway. Her breath caught in her throat and she froze for a moment.

Then, gathering her wits, she continued up the stairs to face her father, Simon Grant. "Hello, Daddy," she said, stopping in front of him.

"Hello, Lucinda," her father murmured.

He was dressed in a suit and tie, his shirt still impeccably pressed even at this late hour of the day. He never really looked human to her when he was in a business suit. She found him much more pliable when he was dressed for riding.

Sunny cleared her throat. "Lucinda? Is that how it's going to be? You only call me Lucinda when you're angry with me. What have I done wrong now?"

"Do you even have to ask?"

"I'm sure you can't wait to tell me."

"You take off with some…some stranger and you don't think you've done anything wrong? No one had any idea where you were or who you were with."

"I called Lily. She knew. I didn't think you cared. I haven't seen you in over a month."

He cursed softly. "Don't be ridiculous."

"Don't call me ridiculous," Sunny said. She wasn't going to let her father bait her into an argument. It always happened this way. He'd goad her into a fight and then he'd spend the following half hour making her feel like an ungrateful child. She drew a deep breath. "Why don't you come inside? I'll get you something to drink."

She walked past him and, to her relief, he followed her inside. Tossing her towel onto the granite countertop, she headed to the refrigerator. "We have beer, orange juice."

"A vodka martini," he said.

"I'm not sure if we—"

"The vodka is in the cabinet above the sink. There should be—" He sighed. "Never mind, I'll make it."

Her father joined her in the kitchen and Sunny pulled out a stool at the breakfast bar and sat down, cupping her chin in her hand. "I didn't realize you had a place here in Adelaide, too, until your assistant offered to let us stay here."

"Us?"

"His name is Logan. Logan Quinn. He's a horse breeder and he has a horse I want."

"And that's why you've decided to run away with him?" Her father tossed some ice in a glass and filled it full of vodka, then threw in a couple of olives.

"I didn't run away. I just needed to…get away. I needed out of that house and he was going somewhere, so I decided to hitch a ride. I figured I could convince him to sell the horse."

"What do you need another horse for? You're not riding the one you have." He took a sip of his vodka and watched her over the rim of his glass.

"Tally is a beautiful horse. And I'd like to train her. Ed has seen her. He agrees." In truth, she wasn't sure that Ed did agree, but he'd be stupid not to.

"That's all this is, then? Some crazy scheme to get a horse you want?"

"Yes," she lied. But as soon as she answered, Sunny felt the guilt set in. She wasn't just lying to her father, she was betraying herself—and Logan. There was more to this than just Tally. So much more. But how was she supposed to explain that to her father?

"Sunny? Is everything all right?"

She spun around on the stool and saw Logan standing in the middle of the room. He slowly approached, his expression curious but guarded.

Sunny drew a deep breath. "Logan Quinn, this is my father, Simon Grant. Daddy, this is Logan."

Logan quickly stepped forward and held out his hand. "Sir, it's a pleasure to meet you."

Reluctantly, her father returned the gesture. "You're the man with the horse? How much is it going to take?"

"Take?" Logan frowned. "Oh, you mean to buy her? She's not for sale. Actually, she's already been sold."

Her father scowled, turning back to Sunny. "The horse is not for sale. You've been running around the countryside with this guy and he has no intention of selling you his horse." He slammed the glass down on the countertop, causing Sunny to jump. "Get your things. We're leaving."

"I'm not," Sunny said sharply.

"Do not try my patience. I can cut you off in a heartbeat."

"Do it," Sunny said. "Go ahead. I don't care. I'll take Padma and I'll leave."

"Padma doesn't belong to you," he said.

"You gave her to me for my twenty-first birthday, don't you remember?"

He strode to the door. "Maybe you need time to think about what you're giving up. I'll expect you in my office first thing in the morning. If you don't show up, you know what will happen."

"Oh, Daddy, please. You threaten me all the time with that. It's getting old."

He turned to Logan. "If you think you're going to benefit from my bank account, you might as well move on to your next target. Sunny doesn't get anything unless it comes through me. I won't have her associating with the likes of you."

With that, her father strode to the door. He slammed it shut behind him, leaving the interior of the villa silent and Sunny stunned. "I—I'm so sorry. He should never have said that. He doesn't know you and he—"

"He's right," Logan said. Crossing the kitchen, he opened the fridge and grabbed a beer, then twisted off the cap. "He's right."

"No, he isn't. He doesn't know anything about you."

"I'm sure he took one look at the campervan and could see everything he needed to know." He shrugged. "It's all right. I understand completely. Hell, if I were him, I wouldn't want my daughter hanging around with a guy like me, either."

"Don't say that," Sunny murmured.

Logan took a long drink of his beer. "It's the truth."

With that, he silently strode back through the villa and out the door to the beach. Sunny watched him leave, knowing that her father's objections were not going to go down well with a man like Logan. If he was anything, he was proud.

She sat down on the stool and grabbed her father's glass of vodka, taking a swallow. "Well, if I'm going to be disowned, I'm going to have to make some plans."

LOGAN STOOD IN KNEE-DEEP water, staring out at the horizon. Every now and then he could spot dolphins in the gulf, breaking the surface. He felt as if he'd been punched in the stomach and he couldn't catch his breath.

He shouldn't have expected a warm reception from Sunny's father, but he certainly didn't anticipate such a hostile reaction. The fact that he assumed Logan was only after her money was a bit hard to reconcile, but it was probably a logical conclusion.

He heard the water splashing behind him and a moment later, Sunny's hand slipped into his. They stood silently for a long time. Logan saw a pair of dolphins and pointed. "See them?"

"What?"

"Dolphins. Just out there. To the right of that big boat."

Sunny held her hand over her eyes and then smiled. "I see them. They look like they're having fun." She laughed softly. "They probably don't have an awful dolphin father telling them what to do every moment of every day."

"He's not awful, Sunny. He's just trying to protect you."

"From what? From you?"

"Yeah. Me and a million other men who might have ulterior motives."

"I'm twenty-six years old," Sunny said. "When do I get to make decisions for myself?"

"I reckon that's up to you," he replied.

"And what if I decided I didn't want to obey my father? What if I decided I didn't want to go home?"

He turned to her, slipping his arms around her waist. "What are you saying?"

"I don't have anywhere to go," she said. "If I left, would you take me in?"

Logan gasped. "What?"

"You heard me. Can I stay with you? Just until I figure out what I want to do with my life. I can help you work the ranch. You know I'm good with horses."

"Sunny, this is not a decision you make lightly. This is your family. What about your riding? I thought you were going to start that again."

"Well, I figured we could steal Padma on our way

back through and take her to your ranch. The two of us could live there."

"You're going to steal a horse from your father?"

Sunny sighed in frustration. "She's my horse. He gave her to me for my twenty-first birthday. There was a huge party. Everyone was there. I have witnesses."

"All right. Let's say we get your horse and we take it to my ranch. How are you going to afford to pay for the travel and the entry fees and everything else that comes with competing on a world-class level?" He fixed his gaze on hers as he waited for her answer. But Logan could tell that there wouldn't be one coming. "You can't ride without your father's help, Sunny. So it seems that you have no choice in the matter."

She spun away from him and trudged through the water, cursing angrily. Logan knew the feeling, being trapped in a life she couldn't seem to escape. But he certainly wasn't going to encourage her any further. He'd been running away from poverty and uncertainty. She was running away from a comfortable life, a life she wouldn't find with him.

"What do you want, Sunny?"

She turned to face him. "I just want to be happy. I want to wake up in the morning and know that I'm going to spend the day doing something I love."

"Isn't that riding?"

Their gazes met and locked for a long moment,

then she shook her head and started down the beach, dragging her feet through the shallow water. Logan watched her retreat and wondered if he ought to go after her.

The thought of her living with him at the ranch was like a dream come true. Every day, waking up beside her. Every night, making love until they fell asleep from exhaustion. Having her with him would make his life complete. But it would only fracture hers. And he couldn't do that to her.

Maybe it was best to let her sort this all out on her own. She knew what she needed to do. She was just angry with her father and looking for a way to punish him.

Logan walked back to the villa and climbed the steps to the terrace. The doors were thrown open, the salty evening breeze thick in the air. He glanced around the interior, taking in the luxurious surroundings. This was the life, Logan mused. Comfortable, relaxed, not a care in the world. Why would anyone give it up voluntarily?

Maybe he should take the easy way out and just leave. It would make Sunny's decision much easier. And they had a long stretch of road ahead of them— the desolate Eyre Highway, a seemingly endless road that connected Southern Australia and Western Australia.

But Logan was too selfish. He wanted her company for this final part of the trip. He needed her there when he finally had to give up Tally to her new owner. He wasn't willing to relinquish a single day of their time together.

He grabbed a beer from the fridge and walked back out on the terrace. The sun was beginning to sink toward the horizon, and he wondered how long she'd be. Logan tried to still the impulse to go find her. He imagined all sorts of trouble she might find along the beach. But his instinct to protect her was tempered with the knowledge that sometimes Sunny just needed to be alone.

He walked back inside the villa and ran his hands through his damp hair. A shower would keep his mind off things, at least until she got back home. He took another sip of his beer and walked into the bedroom, kicking off his shorts along the way.

The shower was just as luxurious as the rest of the villa, lined with pale green glass tile. It was large enough for two, with double showerheads hanging from the ceiling. Logan adjusted the water temperature and stepped inside, his beer still clutched in his hand.

The rush of warm water felt good on his salt-caked skin. Running his hand through his hair, Logan turned his face up to the spray. Unlike the shower at his ranch, this one didn't run out of hot water after five minutes

When he felt arms slip around his waist, he realized that he'd been indulging in the luxury far longer than normal. She pressed her lips to the center of his back, and he slowly turned to face her, capturing her lips in a deep, delicious kiss.

No matter what was said between them, however harsh it might be, they could always come back to this—this sweet and powerful attraction. A kiss, a touch, a simple sigh was all it took to communicate more than an entire conversation.

Logan set the beer on the marble bench in the shower, then smoothed his hands over her naked body. He'd become so familiar with every curve, every perfect feature. There wasn't a spot on her body that his lips hadn't grazed or his fingers hadn't explored. She'd taken her own time learning his body, as well.

Now, when she wrapped her fingers around his hard shaft, Logan knew her touch would set every nerve in his body on fire. She sensed when to caress softly and slowly and when to be more aggressive. And when he reached between her legs and ran his fingers along her damp slit, he knew exactly what would make her writhe and gasp.

There would come a time, in the near future, when he wouldn't have her close, when her kisses and her touch would only be a memory. As she brought him closer to completion, Logan tried to enjoy every sensation, knowing he'd want to recall it all later.

"I love the way you touch me," he whispered, the warm water still falling down over them.

Logan slipped a finger inside her and Sunny moaned as he increased the pressure. Her forehead was pressed against his chest, her hair hiding her face. But as she came closer, she looked up at him, their gazes meeting through the rush of the shower.

She whispered his name once and then dissolved into a series of powerful spasms, her body crumpling against his. Watching her surrender was all he needed to tumble over the edge, and he followed her, her hand growing slick with his seed.

When it was over, Logan pressed her back against the wall of the shower and kissed her, his tongue teasing at her lips, nipping and sucking. "I have to get a shower like this," Logan said. "It never runs out of hot water."

"Oh, I thought it was the naked girl in the shower that you liked."

"Well, I can find one of those anywhere," Logan teased.

She tightened her grip on his shaft. "Really."

"No," he said in a high-pitched voice.

"Good. Because you may find me in your shower occasionally."

"I can live with that," Logan murmured, kissing her again.

So she hadn't changed her mind about moving in with him. He wanted to talk about her plans, to understand why she'd make such a rash decision. They hadn't made any kind of commitment to each other.

They'd talked about the future only in very vague terms. But it seemed, for now, that they actually had a future together.

LOGAN PULLED THE campervan up in front of the Adelaide headquarters for Grant Energies. It was still early in the morning but the street parking had all been taken. Sunny knew her father was inside, probably waiting impatiently for a daughter he never seemed to have time for in the first place. "I'll find a spot," Logan said. "Maybe you better go in. You don't want to keep your father waiting."

Sunny turned to Logan, trying to calm her nerves. "Promise you'll wait for me," she said, ignoring a flutter in her stomach.

"I will. I'm not going anywhere."

"Ten minutes. That's all it will take. I just want to explain to him what I'm doing and try to smooth things out."

Logan nodded. "And if you don't come out?"

"I'll be back," she said. "I promise. Ten minutes. Don't leave." She leaned over and gave him a quick kiss, pressing her palm to his cheek. "Wish me luck."

"Luck," he said.

Sunny forced a smile. "All right. This is going to go well." She reached for the door, then thought better of it and gave him another kiss, this one longer and more intimate. The contact seemed to give her strength. A moment later, she hopped out of the passenger door and hurried to the entrance of the building. She glanced back over her shoulder and gave Logan a wave, then walked inside.

She stopped at the security desk and announced herself, but the guard recognized her from two nights before. As she strode through the spacious lobby, Sunny carefully went through all she planned to say.

The receptionist was waiting behind the desk as she had been that first day, and Sunny wondered whether she ever left—or if she ever stopped smiling.

"Good morning, Miss Grant. Your father is waiting for you in his office. Jennifer is coming up to take you there."

Sunny sat down in one of the chairs, twisting her fingers together in an attempt to still her nerves. A minute ticked by and then another before Jennifer appeared in the lobby. Though she didn't know much about her father's business, it was clear that he enjoyed surrounding himself with attractive employees. His mistress had started off her "career" as his assistant.

"Follow me, Miss Grant. Can I get you anything to drink? Coffee, juice?"

"A large bottle of vodka would be good," Sunny murmured.

"I'm sorry?"

"Never mind. Just a little gallows humor." Sunny pasted a smile on her face. "Thank you for making the arrangements for the villa. I appreciate everything you did."

"Not a problem," she said. "We were happy to host you." Reaching for the knob on a huge wooden door, she opened it and then stepped aside. "It was a pleasure to finally meet you, Miss Grant."

Sunny slowly walked into the office. Her father was sitting at a sleek, modern desk, his gaze fixed on his laptop computer. "Sit," he said.

"I'll stand. I'm not staying long."

Simon Grant glanced up. "I've called a driver. He'll take you to the airport." Her father retrieved an envelope from his pocket and pushed it across his desk. "There's a ticket inside. And some spending money. I'm glad you've seen the error of your ways."

Sunny approached his desk. "What error, Daddy? I had the wonderful luck to find a kind and understanding man. He hasn't had a lot of breaks in his life, but he's hardworking and honest. And I decided I wanted to spend more time with him. And now, I think I'm falling in love with him. I can't, for the life of me, see how that could possibly be an error."

"What do you even know about this man?"

"I know enough. When you decided to cut me off, he told me I could stay with him. He cares about me, without any conditions or expectations." She drew a ragged breath. "We make each other happy."

"You can be so naive, Sunny," her father said, shaking his head.

"I'm not naive, Daddy. I'm optimistic. You taught me to dream big and that's what I'm doing. I believe that I can find a man who'll make me happy for the rest of my life. And I believe we could be deliriously happy. Do you know how amazing that feels? I've watched you and Mom tear each other apart, and yet, I still believe in love. Somewhere, deep inside my heart, that hope didn't really die."

"You're going home," he ordered.

"I'm not. I'm going with Logan. And after that, we're going to drive back to the farm and we're going to pick up my things and Padma and I'm going to live with him."

"You're just going to give it all up? I don't think you will." He opened a drawer in his desk and pulled out a leather-bound book. When he opened it, Sunny knew what was coming next. *Money.* Whenever her father couldn't bend her into submission, he always dangled money in front of her. Well, this time it wasn't going to work.

"How much?" he asked.

"You can't buy me off."

"You wanted that horse. The one he's selling. How much will it take to get it?"

Sunny stifled a gasp. Was he really offering her a chance to buy Tally? Emotion welled up inside her at the thought that she might be able to save Tally for Logan, to save the filly for both of them.

It seemed as if their entire relationship was tied

up around Tally, and the moment they let her go, what they shared together might suddenly dissolve.

"Well? What will it take?"

"I—I don't know." Sunny held her breath. If she took the money, she'd have the horse. But would she be expected to give up Logan in return? Or was there a way to have them both? "I'd have to talk to the owner." She drew a deep breath. "Would she be mine then?"

"As long as you give up this Logan person and rededicate yourself to your riding, you can do whatever you want with the horse." Her father signed the check and handed it to her. "It's blank. Fill in whatever you need. I'll expect you back home by the end of the week and ready to focus. If I don't find you there, I'll stop payment on the check or I'll sell the horse. Do we have an understanding?"

"We do," she murmured. Sunny met his gaze. "Are you happy now?"

"You need to get your life back on track, Sunny. World championships are in two years and Rio is in four. Equestrians can ride for years. You still have a chance to make your dream come true."

"I do," she said. It wasn't a lie. The only problem was, the dream her father spoke of wasn't her dream anymore. At least, not the one that occupied all her thoughts and desires. "Is there anything else?"

He tapped his finger to his temple. "Back on track," he said. "Think like a winner."

"Back on track," she replied.

Sunny glanced over at the clock, then realized she'd been in the office nearly ten minutes. Logan would be waiting downstairs, wondering if she was ever coming back. "I have to go. I'll see you at home."

"We'll go riding," he offered.

Sunny nodded. "Goodbye, Daddy. And thank you. For the money. You won't be disappointed." She walked calmly out the door, tucking the check into her jeans pocket. It took forever to get back to the lobby, weaving through a maze of cubicles and hallways. When she finally reached the reception- ist, she was running.

"I'm late," Sunny called, racing out of the office. She was breathless by the time she got to the street and gazed around, looking frantically for the camp- ervan.

"Logan?" She ran up the block, but there was no sight of him. She should have known he'd leave. He wasn't willing to stand between her and her father and he'd taken the only way out. Sunny stopped and ran her fingers through her hair, tears pushing at the corners of her eyes.

It felt like every bit of energy had just been sapped from her body. Her knees were weak and all she wanted to do was sit down on the sidewalk and have a good cry.

"Sunny?"

The sound of his voice startled her and she spun around to see him walking toward her. With a tiny cry, she ran to him and threw herself into his arms. "I thought you'd gone."

"I couldn't find a place to park. The campervan takes two spots. The last time we were here it was after work hours."

He drew back to look down into her face. "Why are you crying?" With his thumb, he wiped away a tear from her cheek. "I'm not going anywhere."

"Let's go get our horse and get on the road." She drew a ragged breath. "I'm done with this city. We seem to have a better time of it when we're headed somewhere."

When they finally reached the campervan, parked a few blocks away, Logan opened the passenger door for her and helped her inside. "Your carriage awaits," he teased.

As she settled into her seat, Sunny couldn't help but feel a sense of optimism. She had the money to buy back Logan's horse. For now, that was enough. And once Tally was hers, the rest of it would sort itself out.

"Where are we headed today?" Sunny asked as Logan got behind the wheel.

"I don't know. Let's just drive west and see where the road takes us."

Sunny smiled to herself. After a few rocky moments, things were back to normal now. She and

Logan were together in a place that had always been comfortable for them both. All was right with the world.

7

THE LAST THIRD of the trip was the most difficult, spent crossing the Nullarbor Plain, a swath of land that was nothing more than a giant slab of limestone, unable to support any vegetation beyond scrub brush. It was the epitome of Australian outback, desolate and remote.

At times, looking out to the horizon, it seemed as if they were on another planet. There were no houses, no towns, nothing but the straight strip of sealed road in front of them, a thousand kilometers long.

Every two or three hundred kilometers, they'd come upon a roadhouse where they could buy food and get petrol and spend the night if they chose. But Logan had wanted to put that part of the trip behind them as quickly as possible so they did the crossing in two very long days of driving, spending their only night on the border between the two states in Eucla.

Since the road was so straight and virtually void of traffic, Sunny finally got her chance to drive the campervan. Though Logan was reluctant to relinquish control to her, she turned out to be a very good driver, patient while she learned and very careful once she felt comfortable.

After pulling into the Eucla caravan park at almost midnight, they took Tally for a short ride and then got her fed and bedded down for the night. They were back on the road again early the next morning, this time hugging the coast and spending the night near Albany.

It was their last night with Tally, and Logan had decided that the final four-hour drive to Perth could wait until the afternoon. He was determined to spend the morning riding and taking his last chance to say goodbye to his favorite filly.

They found a caravan park near a small beach and left the campervan and trailer, leading Tally to the long stretch of white sand. She seemed to sense that something was wrong and, as they walked, continued to nudge at Logan's shoulder.

"I think she knows," Sunny said, looking up at him.

He held her hand, clasped in his, and gave it a squeeze. "I think she does, too," he said. "But I have to believe she'll be fine."

"Of course she will," Sunny said.

"I hope they'll appreciate what they have. I mean,

she was the most beautiful horse in my stable. I always liked walking in every morning and seeing her head peeking over the stall door, looking for her morning biscuit."

"And she'll be the most beautiful horse in their stable."

When they reached the beach, Logan gave Sunny a knee up and then jumped up behind her, settling Sunny against him. They rode without a saddle, the two of them as comfortable riding together as they were riding alone.

After two long days on the road, Tally was full of energy and ready to run. Logan urged her into a gallop and they ran along the edge of the surf, the horse's hooves sending spray up all around them.

They rode until they were both exhausted, then walked along the beach as Tally cooled down. There was nothing to say, and Logan was grateful that Sunny hadn't tried to brighten his mood. In truth, she seemed almost as sad as he was.

He always thought he might take the option of selling the horse to Sunny. It was a last-minute escape clause in case he couldn't go through with the sale. But now that she'd cut off ties with her father, that was impossible. The sale would go as originally planned.

"So, are we ready to turn around and go home?" Sunny asked.

Logan nodded. "Yeah. I think we can get back a

lot faster. We can put in longer days, maybe just pull off the road when we need sleep. If I can keep this trip to two weeks, it would probably be a good idea."

"We'll have to stop and get Padma," Sunny said. "And pick up my things."

"Sunny, are you sure you want to do this? Maybe you should go home and try to smooth things over with your dad. We'll just keep to our plan of taking a holiday every now and then."

She stopped walking and turned to face him. "Don't you want me to live with you?"

"Of course I do. That's not the point. The point is, are you going to want to live with me? I don't have anywhere for you to train. And it takes hours to get to the closest equestrian park. I don't even know where the closest one is."

"We can build some fences. It's not that difficult."

"Sunny, come on. I just want you to understand what you'd be giving up. If you're really serious about riding at Worlds in a couple years, you're not going to get there living on my ranch."

She stared at him for a long moment, then sighed softly. "I know." Sunny pushed up on her toes and kissed his cheek. "But thank you for offering to take me in. If I ever feel like running away, I might show up on your doorstep."

"I could handle that," he said.

"We will see each other after this is over," she

said. "I'm not even sure I'm going to be able to sleep all alone again. I've gotten used to having you there."

Logan chuckled, wrapping his arm around her shoulders and pulling her close. "You have managed to wiggle your way into my life. I don't think there's any getting rid of you now."

"Absolutely not," she said.

He handed her the reins. "Here. Take her for one last ride. I want to watch you."

"Should I take off all my clothes like Lady Godiva?" Sunny asked, looking up and down the beach. "We're all alone here."

"Only if you're determined to make me cry," Logan teased. He held his linked hands out and gave her a boost and Sunny gathered the reins in her fingers.

"Are you sure you don't want to come along?" she asked.

"No, I just want to look at my two favorite girls for a little bit longer."

Sunny clucked her tongue as she gave the horse a gentle nudge with her heels. Logan stepped back and sat down in the sand, resting his arms across his knees.

He wished he'd had a camera with him so he could keep a memory of this moment in time. He reached into his pocket and looked at his mobile phone, then realized that he did have a camera.

He pointed it at Sunny and Tally and snapped a

picture, then squinted to see it on the phone's display. After he saved it, Logan noticed that he'd had a call from Billy at the ranch. Logan had promised that he was going to contact him when he got to Perth, but there was obviously something Billy needed and wasn't willing to wait.

Logan punched in the number for the ranch, then listened as the phone rang six times before the voice mail kicked in. "Hey, Billy. I noticed that you called. I'm in mobile range right now, so ring me back. I hope everything is all right. I just got to Perth and will be dropping Tally off this afternoon. All right, then. Get back to me when you can."

With a frown, he hung up and stared at his mobile, wondering what Billy wanted. He'd worked for Logan for three years and had always been trustworthy and responsible. Logan also had a couple of local boys who were working the place in return for using a couple of horses for amateur camp drafting competitions.

Sunny approached him, Tally at a brisk walk. "Hey, I thought you were going to watch me. You're playing with your mobile."

Logan held it up and snapped another photo of her. "That was a nice one," he said.

"Take one of us together," she said.

Logan got to his feet and Sunny bent over Tally's neck. He held out his arm and snapped the picture, then showed it to her. "I like that one," she said. "You'll have to send me that so I have a copy."

"I will," he said.

"What is it? You look worried."

"No. Billy called and I guess I must have turned off my phone, because I didn't hear him ring. He wouldn't call unless there was some type of emergency."

"Did you ring him back?"

Logan nodded. "Yeah. He didn't answer. I'm thinking I should try one of the other boys, but they only come by after they're done with school. They might not know what's going on."

He frowned. "He's got a mobile. Maybe I should text him. I'll just tell him to call me." Logan typed in a quick text then waited, hoping that he'd ring right back. But as they stood there, staring at the phone, he realized, even if there was an emergency, he was at least five days away from being able to help.

"Maybe we should get going," he said. "If there's something wrong, I'm going to have to head back right away."

"All right," she said. "But hop up on Tally. I want to take a photo of you."

Logan did as she asked and Sunny stood back and snapped the picture. "There," she murmured. "That's perfect."

She turned the phone to him and Logan nodded.

"That is nice. I think I might have to frame that one and put it up in my stable."

"I'll frame it for you," Sunny said. "And the one of us together. It will be a good memory of our trip."

"I don't think I'm going to be forgetting this trip anytime soon."

Sunny grinned as he slipped off Tally's back and drew her into a slow heated kiss. "Good. I don't want you to forget a single moment."

THOUGH SUNNY HAD BEEN happy to delay the inevitable, she knew they were due to deliver the filly to the equine vet by three that afternoon. The new owner would be waiting to pick her up and the sale would be finalized.

Since her fight with her father, she'd stopped trying to convince Logan that she'd be a better owner. The closer they got to Perth, the gloomier his mood seemed to become. So she'd dropped the subject and, instead, Sunny had decided to bide her time, the blank check from her father tucked securely in her pocket. If Logan was so determined to go through with the sale, then she'd have to work around him.

Years of getting her way with her father had trained her to look for every available option, and she still had plenty. In the worst case, her blank check would be turned down. Then she'd go home, have Ed call and make another offer for Tally and keep negotiating until they finally said yes. Tally wasn't going anywhere, and Sunny had enough money to keep tempting them with better offers.

They found the equine vet without any trouble. His practice was located about thirty kilometers outside of Perth, not far off the coast highway.

Logan slowed to pull into the car park. "I feel like I should just keep driving. Make a big circle around Oz and end up back at home."

"We could do that," she said. "Just keep going, I won't talk you out of it."

Logan shook his head. "Nope. I breed horses. And I sell horses. I'm all right with that."

They followed a driveway around to the back of the equine clinic and found a small barn with a white-fenced paddock attached to it. Logan pulled the campervan to a stop and turned off the ignition, then reached down for the envelope that contained the horse's medical information and breeding papers.

"Do you want me to come with you?" she asked.

He opened his mouth to answer, then sighed softly and closed it. His hand rested on the steering wheel, and Sunny watched as his fingers clenched and unclenched. "You take her in," Logan finally said.

"Me?"

He nodded. "I can't do it. Once the vet has looked her over, you'll get the check and then we'll be on our way. I don't need to be there."

"Are you sure?" she asked.

He drew another deep breath. "I've never been

surer of anything in my life. I want my last memory of Tally to be on that beach, watching the two of you ride through the surf. I'd be happy with that."

Sunny leaned over and gently kissed him. "You'll be all right. I promise."

He gave her a weak smile. "I know. I'm going to have to get used to this." Logan handed her the envelope. "Say goodbye for me, will you?"

"I will," she murmured. She gave him another long, sweet kiss before she hopped out of the campervan. She walked around to the back of the trailer and lowered the ramp, then unlatched the door.

"Hey, sweetheart," she crooned as she moved beside the horse, stroking her back. "Come on, you and I have some business to take care of." The horse looked at her with a quizzical gaze. "I know. It's been a long trip. But if you're willing to travel just a little bit farther, then you and I are both going to get exactly what we want."

Gripping the halter, she slowly nudged Tally back, guiding her out of the trailer onto firm ground. After over a week on the road, the horse seemed to take the travel in stride. Her ears perked up and she sniffed the air, getting her bearings again before walking beside Sunny to the gate.

She rang a bell on the gatepost, and a few minutes later, the equine vet came out, tugging his hat on his head against the afternoon sun. He was followed by an older man, dressed in jeans and a cotton shirt.

"Hello," the vet said. "Is this Tally?"

Sunny nodded. "It is. I understand you're going to look her over and I'm supposed to give these to the new owner and collect a check."

"I'm here for Mr. Morton," the man in the plaid shirt said. "Beck Crenshaw. I'm his stable manager."

"Then you're the man I need to talk to," Sunny said, grabbing his arm. "Will you excuse us?"

The vet nodded and started his examination, running his hands over the horse's front legs.

"Is there something wrong?" Crenshaw asked.

"There is. I want to buy the horse," Sunny said.

"That horse?"

She nodded. "Yep. I know what you're paying for the horse. I'll give you that and twenty thousand more to buy her back."

Crenshaw laughed. "You have to be joking. You just drove that horse across country and now you want to turn around and take her right back?"

"No, I'm going to board her on your farm for a week and then we're going to put her on a plane and send her back to Brisbane."

"And you're going to pay me almost twice as much as she's worth." Crenshaw stared at her for a long moment, shaking his head. "Wait a second. You're Sunny Grant, aren't you?"

"I am. But don't hold that against me."

"And you want to buy *this* horse?"

"I do. I think I'm offering you a very fair price. Can we come to an agreement?"

He chuckled. "Hell, yeah, I think we can make a deal," he said. "I'm in the business of buying and selling horses. If there's a profit to be made, I'll take it."

"All right, then," Sunny said. "It's a deal. Forty-four thousand plus boarding for a week. Now, do you have a mobile? I left mine at home."

He handed her his phone and she punched in the number for the stable office at Willimston Farm. When Ed answered, she drew a deep breath. "Ed, this is Sunny. I'm going to put you on the phone with a Mr. Crenshaw. I want you to make some travel arrangements to bring Logan's filly back to Wil-limston. I've offered him forty-four thousand, which is probably more than we'd normally pay, but I don't care. I'm going to give him another five thousand for board and airfare. Can you do that for me?"

"Sunny, what the hell are you—"

"Just do this for me. I've worked out all the de-tails with my father. You know I'm right about this horse. I know you know."

"All right. Let me talk to the man."

Sunny smiled at Beck. "You have a check for me, right?"

He reached in his pocket and withdrew an en-velope. "This is the easiest money I've ever made selling a horse."

Sunny filled out her father's check and exchanged it with him. "It was a pleasure doing business with you." She handed him the phone. "Ed Perkins is our stable manager. He'll help you make travel arrangements for Tally."

"Are you going to train her to jump?" Crenshaw asked, nodding at the filly.

"I'm not sure. I haven't decided what I'm going to do."

Sunny shook his hand and then turned and walked back to the campervan. She closed the trailer doors and stowed the ramp, then walked around to the passenger side. Logan was inside, still sitting behind the wheel, his hat pulled down low over his eyes. He looked over at her and she could see him fighting back tears.

"We're done," she said. She handed him the check. "Make sure it's right before we leave."

He opened the envelope and peered inside. "It's right."

"Then let's go," she said. "I'll buy you dinner and we'll rent a pricey hotel room. And then maybe, you and I will get a little bit stonkered."

"All right," he said. "That sounds perfect. I'm a rich man now. I can afford a few extra luxuries."

"Oh, no, this is my treat," she said. "We're going to find a place that has room service, we're going to take a nice long shower and then we're going to order dinner. I'm going to spend my money before my daddy puts a stop on my bank card. And after dinner, we're going to curl up in bed and I'm going to seduce you very, very slowly."

He drew a ragged breath. "I really am glad you're here with me, Sonny," he said.

"Are you happy you didn't desert me in Adelaide?"

He chuckled softly. "Yes. That was not my finest moment. I was just feeling a little…overwhelmed."

"And what about now?" Sunny asked. "Does all this still scare you?"

Logan leaned back and closed his eyes. "Yeah, it does," he said. "Right now, I'm the saddest I've been in a long time, but I'm happier than I can ever remember. Does that make sense?"

"No, but I'm sure you'll figure it all out. Come on, let's go."

Logan started up the campervan and they drove out of the car park and onto the highway. Sunny held out her hand and he placed his palm against hers, weaving their fingers together. "It feels different," he said. "Driving with the empty trailer."

"Maybe you'll let me drive again on the way home?"

"I think that can be arranged."

Sunny tried to keep the conversation light as they drove into Perth and searched for a place to stay. He might feel sad now, but there would come a day when she'd give him everything he ever wanted and needed. For now, she'd look forward to that moment and not worry about anything else.

SUNNY SLIPPED THE KEY CARD into the lock and waited for the light as Logan looked over her shoulder. His hands spanned her waist as she opened the door to the room and he gently pushed her inside, dropping their bags on the floor along the way.

He'd been waiting for this since the moment they'd left the vet's, and he stumbled with her toward the bed, his mouth searching for hers. Caught in a long, desperate kiss, they tore at each other's clothes.

There was nothing to say that they couldn't say with a touch or a sigh. He needed to be close to her, to possess her. It would reassure him that everything was still all right, because it suddenly felt as if the world was out of balance.

She worked at the button on the front of his jeans and when it was finally undone, Sunny smoothed her hand beneath the waistband of his underdaks. Wrapping her fingers around his shaft, she began to stroke him.

It was all Logan needed. There was a comfort in the intimacy, the way she knew his body and what made him ache with desire. This was what he had to keep, this feeling, this woman who had captured his heart. Horses would come and go, but he couldn't afford to lose Sunny.

He cupped her face in his hands, molding her

mouth to his, tasting deeply of her sweet lips. The need was overwhelming, and he wanted that perfect moment, when he buried himself deep inside her heat. That had become home to him.

Together, they stripped away the last of their clothes. When she stood naked in front of him, he drew her leg up along his hip, the tip of his shaft teasing at her entrance. He was already on the edge and Logan had to focus on the feel of her hair between his fingers, the sound of her sighs as he kissed her.

Everything he'd ever wanted was here in front of him. He'd always felt like home was a place, a house, a piece of property. But he now knew the truth of love. Home was wherever that one person was. That's what had kept his parents together, through all the troubles.

He could be happy with her anywhere, even living out of the campervan. But he wanted to give her a life she could depend upon. He needed to know she'd be safe with him—forever.

Sunny wriggled against him, the warm flesh of her breasts pressed against his chest. When she slipped her arms around his neck, Logan grabbed her waist and pulled her up against him. With her legs wrapped around him, he pressed her back against the wall.

"Tell me what you want," he murmured.

"You," she breathed, gasping as he entered her. "It will always be you."

She moaned as she sank down on top of him, burying him deep inside her. Logan held on to her hips, his self-control wavering. But this time, he didn't want it to end. He needed this wave of sensation to continue on, an endless surge that could last a lifetime.

He'd never known passion like this, never known it was even possible to feel so deeply for a woman. Grabbing her hand, he kissed it then clasped it behind her as he began to move.

At first, the rhythm was slow and deep, but as he saw her dancing closer to her release, he knew she needed more. He drew away, nearly breaking the intimate contact, and then brought her down on him quickly.

Sunny gasped as he thrust again, his pace increasing until she writhed against him, her cries of pleasure echoing in his ears. And then, her body tensed and it was all over. Sunny dissolved into deep and powerful spasms, spasms that sent fresh waves of pleasure coursing through his body.

When she was sated, she opened her eyes and looked at him. And that was all it took for Logan to reach his own orgasm. He drove into her one last time and then let himself go, his body shuddering, his legs barely strong enough to keep them both upright.

"I think I might fall down," he murmured.

"I don't want to move right now."

He slipped his hands beneath her backside, and

he carried her over to the bed then gently set her down, stretching out beside her. Logan reached up and brushed a strand of flaxen hair from her eyes, tucking it behind her ear.

"Remember when you told me that we were just friends—friends with benefits?"

"Vaguely," Sunny said. She smiled. "I don't remember it all that clearly since I'd had a little too much wine, but I do recall throwing that wine bottle at you. Why do you bring it up?"

"What does that mean?"

"Friends with benefits?"

"I know what that means. What does it mean for us? Do we see each other when we can and then see other people on the side? Or are we kind of... together?"

"Why do we need to define it?" Sunny asked.

"Maybe I'm feeling insecure," he said.

"You? I thought you were a rock."

He pressed his forehead to hers, closing his eyes. "Don't tease about this. I'm about to get serious here."

"All right," she said.

He heard a tremor in her voice and he opened his eyes. "I used to think that this would end after a few weeks and we'd both go on with our lives. But now, I realize that maybe this is a beginning for us."

"You do?"

"I don't have a lot to offer you, Sunny. And I'd

like you to seriously consider the consequences of leaving your father's house and taking up with me. Not that I wouldn't love having you. In fact, having you with me would be like a dream come true. But living at the ranch would limit your chances to make your dreams come true." He paused. "If you decide to stay at home, I'll understand. It won't change the way I feel. Ever."

"How would it work?"

"We could see each other every now and then. I don't expect any type of commitment and I'd understand if you didn't want to, but if you did, I—"

"Yes," she said.

"Yes? Yes to what?"

"Yes, to whatever you want."

"Just like that?"

Sunny sighed. "Yes. I don't want this to be over, either. You can come and visit, I can come and visit. Maybe we can think about the holiday idea again."

"I'd like that," he said.

She leaned into him and touched her lips to his. "Me, too."

"What's the first thing you're going to do when you get home?" he asked.

"I'm going to ride Padma," she said. "I haven't ridden her since London. I just couldn't bring myself to do it. I want to start training, but this time I'm going to really focus. And I'm thinking that I might want to start eventing. I used to do dressage, but I wasn't patient enough to be good at it. But I've changed. I have more perspective now. And I feel I need to challenge myself more. The World championships are in France in two years and then the Olympics in four years in Rio. I could be ready. I could be better than I ever was."

"I know you could," Logan said.

"Do you?"

"Sunny, I think you could do just about anything you set your mind to. You got me to—" He stopped suddenly. He was about to tell her that he'd fallen hopelessly in love with her. How was it possible that those words had come so naturally that he could say them without even thinking?

Was he in love with Sunny? Yes. Did he want to spend the rest of his life with her? Yes. Was he going to tell her that now? Logan drew a deep breath. Probably not the best time.

"What?" she asked.

Logan dropped a quick kiss on her lips. "You got me to haul you across the country just so you could get away for a week or two."

Sunny laughed. "I did. And you almost threw me out on the road that first day. Aren't you glad you kept me?"

"Yeah," he conceded. "We've done all right together."

She grew silent for a long moment, her fingers

tracing lazy patterns on his chest. "I want you to know that you'll be the only one."

"The only one for what?" Logan asked.

"My only one. As long as you want, it's just going to be you. In my bed." She drew a deep breath. "There won't be other men."

Logan stared down at her face but she continued to trace patterns on his chest. "Are you—is that—practical?"

Her shoulders rose in a tiny shrug. "It's the way I want it. What about you?" She risked a glance up. "Are you sure you want it that way?"

Her eyes were wide and questioning and he knew that this was probably the most important moment in their relationship so far. They were making a commitment to each other, vague as it might be. "Yes, that's what I want, too."

"Good," Sunny said. "Then I guess we're kind of…going together."

"Going together," he repeated. He wasn't exactly sure what that meant, only that they'd just promised that they wouldn't have sex with anyone else. As far as he was concerned, Logan wouldn't have any trouble keeping that promise, since he hadn't had much of a sex life since he moved to the ranch.

But Sunny was a different story. She'd have more opportunities. Men noticed women as beautiful as she was, and that kind of attention could turn to attraction…which could easily lead to seduction. After all, she'd seduced him, hadn't she?

"There is one thing," Logan said.

"What is that?"

"If you change your mind, I want you to tell me. Don't avoid me if I ring you up. Don't pretend that everything is all right. Just be straight with me and let me know you've moved on. Can you do that?"

"Don't you trust me?" she asked.

"Of course I do. It's not you I'm worried about. It's all the other men in the world who will see you the way I do. As a beautiful, sexy, irresistible woman."

"All right, I promise," she said.

It was the best he could hope for, Logan mused. Until he had more to offer Sunny, he'd have to be satisfied. But he wasn't going to fool himself. She'd move on, to someone more geographically available, someone with a bigger bank account, maybe even someone her father approved of. And that was all right by him.

Logan was lucky to have her at all. And he'd enjoy the time they had together for as long as it lasted.

8

SUNNY OPENED HER EYES slowly, snuggling deeper into the expensive linens on the hotel bed. She loved waking up next to Logan. They'd been together just over a week and it already seemed like the most natural thing in the world to lie naked beside him. She moved to the middle of the bed, searching for the warmth of his body, but when she couldn't find it, Sunny sat up and looked around the room.

He was standing at the window, looking down on the view of the river as the sun rose, his expression pensive. She studied him in silence, taking in his naked form, the long limbs muscled by hard work, the wide back and shoulders and narrow waist, so masculine, so perfect.

"Are you up already?" she asked softly.

He turned to look at her. "I wanted to call the

ranch and make sure everything was all right. And to let Billy know we'd be on our way back today."

"And everything isn't all right?" she asked, watching him intently.

Logan shook his head. "Billy said there was a guy who stopped by the ranch who insisted on speaking with me. Something about official business. And when Billy said he could call me, the man said that he had to speak to me in person. He had to verify my identity. He said he had very important news about my family and an inheritance. He refused to tell him any more details." Logan cursed softly. "I'm afraid that— No, I don't even want to go there."

"How long has it been since you've heard from your parents?"

"I don't know. Maybe a year. I haven't seen them since right after I bought the ranch. I tried to get them to come and stay with me, but they refused. I can't keep track of them, it's all but impossible. So instead, I just wait until they decide to contact me."

"Do you think something has happened?"

He closed his eyes and drew a deep breath, then let it out. "Yeah, I do."

Sunny crawled out of bed and joined him at the window, slipping her arms around his waist and pressing her body against his. "Then you need to get home," she said. "You need to get on a plane and go. You can fly back to Brisbane and take a bush plane the rest of the way. Do you have a landing strip near the ranch?"

"There's one in town. Billy can come and pick me up."

"Then that's what you'll do," she said.

"Yeah. First, I have to find a place to cash this check. I don't have enough on the bank card for a ticket and a bush plane. And then I'd need to fly back here to pick up the trailer and campervan. Unless I just sell them both."

"No, you don't have to do that. I'll drive them back."

He turned to face her, his fingers toying with a strand of hair that hung over her eyes. "You? Sunny, the drive was difficult for me. I can't ask you to do that. Especially not alone."

"I want to. I'm not ready to go home yet and I'd like to see a little bit more of the country. I might just continue on around and make one big circle. Hey, it could be an adventure."

He chuckled softly. "I think you've had enough adventure."

"I can do this, Logan. Trust me. I promise I'll take my time. And I'll be very careful."

He considered her offer for a long moment and at first, she was certain he'd refuse. But Logan finally shrugged. "All right. But I want you to go home the way we came. You know the route and where to stop along the way. And I don't like you pulling that trailer. I'm thinking you can leave it here and we can figure out a way to get it back. Or I'll just sell it."

Sunny hugged him tight, happy that he was allowing her to help him. He was a proud man, but not too proud to appear vulnerable to her. He trusted her and that meant more than anything to her. "Why don't I call and get a ticket, and then you can take me out for some driving lessons before you leave."

"I don't like this," Logan warned. "You should just fly home with me."

"I don't want to go home yet."

"Then I should stay and we'll drive back together," he countered.

Sunny rolled her eyes. "Are you saying I'm not capable of taking care of myself?" she asked, feeling her temper rise.

Logan paused. "No?"

"Good answer," she said. "Now, bring me your mobile and let's make some travel arrangements. Then, we'll have breakfast and I'll drive you to the airport."

Sunny spent the next half hour making arrangements for Logan to catch a Qantas flight that morning. She gave the agent her bank card info and carefully wrote down the itinerary on a hotel notepad. When she'd confirmed it all, she handed him back his mobile.

"You leave at ten. It's a direct flight from Perth to Brisbane."

"How will I get home from there?"

"I'm going to call my father's pilot. He's usually at my disposal, so he'll fly you. You should be home before dark."

He shook his head. "Thank you. I don't know what to say. I'll pay you back as soon as I get home."

"You don't have to say anything. You can pay me back when I see you the next time," she said. "It's not like I don't know where to find you." She paused. "Actually, I don't really know where to find you."

"I'll draw you a map before I leave." He reached up and smoothed his hand over her cheek. "You're an amazing woman, Sunny Grant."

"Watch me try to convince my father's pilot to fly you out of Brisbane. Then you can tell me I'm amazing."

Sunny sat cross-legged on the bed as she called the number for the small hangar at Brisbane. She usually flew on the company plane to her equestrian events, so she had the number memorized. Once the last leg of his trip was confirmed, she held out the mobile to Logan. He crawled onto the bed and pulled her down beside him.

Sunny leaned over and smoothed her fingers over his furrowed brow. "Don't worry. It might not be anything. You don't know."

"I can feel it," he said. "It's like when my brother died. I got a phone call and my roommate answered.

They wouldn't say anything to him. They'd only talk to me."

She drew his body close to hers. It was hard to know what to say. She'd never really lost anyone close to her. Though her parents were estranged, they were both still alive. And her grandparents were all gone before she turned five.

Running her hands through his hair, she placed a kiss on his lips. "I want you to ring me when you get home tonight," she said.

"How?"

"I'll keep your mobile."

He nodded. "All right. And if you have any trouble along the way, you ring me."

"All right."

"I don't want to leave you, Sunny. I don't like the thought of you driving back through the Nullarbor all by yourself."

"I've learned so much on this trip, but I think I need a little more time to myself. It will be good for me. I have the mobile and plenty of music to listen to. And I'll be back before you know it."

He drew another deep breath and then let it out slowly. "I thought we'd have another week together. I didn't think it would end so quickly."

Sunny stared into his pale blue eyes. She saw fear there, but she wasn't sure what had caused it. Was it what awaited him at home or was it leaving her? "It's not over," she said. "We'll see each other next week.

I have to bring back your campervan and trailer. And I can see your ranch and check out your horses. And maybe hang about for a few days."

"That makes me feel better," he murmured.

"Now, we can either go out and get some breakfast or we can spend the next hour in bed. Which would you prefer?" Sunny asked.

"I'd rather lie here looking at you. Memorizing the color of your eyes and the way your nose wrinkles when you smile."

Sunny kissed him and, gradually, their passion overwhelmed them. This time, when he entered her, it was a sweet, slow experience. It was as if he were savoring every moment, trying to commit it to memory.

She'd never expected to fall in love. When she'd driven off with Logan Quinn, it had been on a lark, just something to do with a few wasted weeks. But now, looking back on their time together, she realized that this trip had been a turning point for her.

She suddenly knew what she wanted out of life and she was ready to make it happen. Though she wasn't sure how she planned to go about it, at least she knew. And though Sunny couldn't figure out all the details right now, she had complete confidence that her life had changed for the better.

After they'd both found their release, they stayed in bed, talking softly about the experiences they'd shared on their road trip. It had become so easy between them and, though they'd had a few ups and downs, Sunny had never felt their disagreements threatened the bond that had formed between them.

It was odd to think that she had a boyfriend now. She'd never had an official boyfriend. There had been men in her life, but never any commitment on her part. But this time it was different. This time, she was determined to make it work.

THE PICKUP TRUCK SENT a plume of dust into the air behind them as they bumped along the narrow road to the ranch house. Billy had come to pick him up from the airstrip near town, and they'd passed the half-hour drive in a detailed interrogation, Logan asking the questions and Billy doing his best to answer them.

"I told him you'd be back late, but he said he'd hang around and wait," Billy said. "When I left he was just sitting in his car reading a book."

"And you're sure he said it was about an inheritance?"

"I—I think so. I really can't remember. He kind of scares the piss out of me. I think he might be from the government."

"And he didn't want to ring me? You're sure of that?"

"Yes, that's one thing I do remember. He said he had to talk to you in person."

"Tell me again exactly what he asked," Logan prodded.

"Mostly things about your family. He knew your dad's name is Daniel and your mom's Lizbeth. And he knew about your brother."

A stab of fear shot through him, and Logan had to remind himself to breathe. What else could this be? It had to be some news about his parents. And the fact that the visitor was unwilling to tell him over the phone didn't bode well.

Logan had always wondered how it would feel to be completely alone in the world. He knew the day would come when his parents weren't around anymore, but he hadn't expected it to happen so soon. If it were his father, then his choice would be obvious. He'd bring his mother to live here at the ranch.

But if it was his mother, he knew his father would never want to settle down in one place for more than a few months.

"Maybe it's not bad news," Billy said. "Maybe... maybe some uncle you didn't know has died and he's leaving you a million dollars."

"I don't have an uncle," he said. "My da was an only child."

"Maybe you won the lotto and don't know it," Billy suggested.

Logan shook his head. Billy had always been an optimistic chap, always looking for the silver lining in every dark cloud. But this dark cloud refused to go away. "Do you think he's still waiting?"

"I'd expect so," Billy said. "This guy is really a bit of a pest. He's not giving up easily."

He'd spent the flight back thinking about Sunny. It had taken every ounce of his determination to leave her at the airport. But she hadn't seemed sad to see him go. In truth, Logan sensed that she was looking forward to the last leg of her adventure. They'd stocked the campervan with food and supplies, she'd recharged the mobile and tested it out, and he'd filled the tank with petrol, warning her not to let it get down below a quarter tank.

Hell, he already missed her. He'd started missing her the moment he walked through the entrance doors at the airport. But it wasn't just a sense of loss that he felt. It was more an emptiness inside of him, as if her presence in his life had become part of who he was.

Where was she right now? he wondered. If she'd left Perth directly after dropping him at the airport, she was probably close to her planned destination in Esperance on the southern coastline. Logan glanced at his watch. She'd promised to call once she stopped for the evening. He needed to hear the sound of her voice now more than ever.

"Did you have a good time?" Billy asked.

His words startled Logan out of his contemplation. "What?"

"A good time? Did you at least have a good time? You haven't been on holiday in…well, since I've come to work here on the ranch. Did you—"

"Yeah," Logan said. "I had a very nice time. The best."

As they came into view of the house, Billy pointed in the direction of a dark sedan. "There it is. I told you he was persistent. That's his car. And that's him, there, sitting on the porch."

Logan stopped the pickup truck and slowly got out. Billy followed close behind him. "You want me to back you up here?" he murmured.

"No, I think I'll be good," Logan said.

As he walked closer, the stranger stood and pasted a smile on his face. "Are you Logan Quinn?" he asked.

Logan stopped, crossing his arms over his chest. He didn't like the look of this guy. Though he was trying to appear friendly, it was obvious he was nervous. "Billy said you wanted to talk to me."

"I do," he said. "I've been waiting around for a couple days now. That Billy. He's a very loyal employee."

"Can I help you with something, Mr.…"

"Winthrop. Arthur Winthrop of the firm of Capley and Drummond in Brisbane. I'm representing Ian Stephens, who represents your great-aunt Aileen Quinn." He paused. "The author."

Logan frowned, the man's words making no sense to him at all. "You're not here about my parents?"

"Do you know where they are? I've been trying to locate them, as well. They're also in line to receive a portion of Miss Quinn's estate."

"Then they're all right?" Logan asked in relief. "My parents are all right? Nothing has happened?"

Arthur blinked. "Not that I know of. As I said, I haven't been able to find them—"

Logan stepped back, shaking his head. "I don't understand. I don't have a great-aunt."

"You do. She's your grandfather's sister and she lives in Ireland. The family was split apart many years ago. She's quite a famous author and now that she's aware of you, she'd like to meet you and to leave you part of her estate. She wants to bequeath you a million dollars, half of which you'll get right now, the other half upon her passing."

The words hit Logan like a punch to the stomach. He gasped, then realized how ridiculous it sounded. "Right. This is some kind of joke." He glanced around. "Where are the cameras? You guys should be ashamed of yourselves. I mean, how low—"

"Mr. Quinn, I'm quite serious. Your great-aunt is extremely wealthy and doesn't have children of her own. She wants to make sure her family benefits from her good fortune. When we find your father, he will also receive a share, and any other surviving heirs of Tomas Quinn. I've confirmed that you are an heir." He reached in his jacket pocket. "This is half of your inheritance. There is only one condition. Miss Quinn wants you to visit Ireland to meet her. Of course, we'll make all the arrangements for you."

Logan closed his eyes. Was he really supposed to believe this? He looked down at the check. It appeared to be real. He recognized the name of the bank and it was written out to him. "What does she want me to do with this?"

"Whatever you want." He glanced around. "It looks like this place could use some improvements. I'm sure this will go a long way. Now, if you'll just sign here."

He held out a paper and Logan added his name to the bottom. "That's it? You're handing me a half-million dollars and that's it?"

"If you don't mind, Mr. Stephens has asked that I take a photo?" He withdrew a digital camera from his pocket. "May I?"

Logan glanced over at Billy then shrugged. "For a half-million dollars? Snap away."

When Winthrop was finished, he handed Logan a business card. "Just ring my number when you're interested in visiting your great-aunt. I'd suggest you do it soon as she is ninety-six years old. Good day, Mr. Quinn, and good luck."

With that, he turned and walked back to his car. A few moments later, he disappeared down the driveway in a plume of dust. Logan stared down at the check, then flipped it over and examined the back. It looked real. But things like this didn't happen to Logan Quinn. He'd had to fight for every single thing he'd ever been given in life.

"Holy dooley, Logan," Billy muttered. "If I'd have known that's what he wanted, I would have called you a lot sooner."

"I can't believe this." Logan laughed. "It's like my future just fell out of the sky and landed at my feet. Do you know what this means?"

"We can afford to fix up the stables?"

"We can afford to sell this place and buy something that's closer to civilization. We can buy a farm with a stable that isn't falling to pieces and a house that doesn't have a leaky roof. A place we can be proud of."

"I'm proud of this place," Billy said, frowning. "We've worked hard here."

Logan nodded. "We have. And someone else who's just starting out will love this place. But, Billy, it's time to move on."

"Are you firing me?"

"No, I'm saying you and I are going to start looking at real estate first thing tomorrow morning." He paused. "And once we get settled, I'm going to buy Tally back. I can offer them whatever they want. She'll be back with us, back on our place."

As he smoothed his fingers over the check, he

realized there were other things that wealth could afford him.

Billy grinned. "You think maybe we could get one of those big-screen televisions? Then I wouldn't have to watch football on that thing you call a television."

"I'll put a television in the barn if you want," Logan said. "You can watch football while you're mucking out the stalls."

"Really?"

Logan grinned. "I think we're going to need to spend carefully," he said. "I have to make a few phone calls and then tomorrow, we're going to the bank to deposit this check, before someone changes their mind."

Logan grabbed his rucksack from the pickup and turned toward the house. As he approached the place that he'd called home for the past five years, he stopped to examine the ramshackle house. He'd grown attached to this place. But now he realized that his home wasn't a spot on a map or a structure made of lumber and nails.

His home was anywhere Sunny Grant was. For the first time, he could imagine a future, a real future, with her. With the money he'd been given, he could buy a nice place, closer to Brisbane, maybe near Willimston Farm. She wouldn't have to make the choice between a life with him or a life pursuing her Olympic dreams.

They could be together. And maybe, when the

time was right, he'd ask her if she'd want to spend the rest of her life with him. He jogged up the porch steps and opened the screen door. For now, he'd keep his plans to himself. And maybe, when Sunny arrived at the ranch next week, he'd be ready to share them.

He walked to the phone and dialed the number to his mobile. It rang six times before the voice mail picked up. It had been almost nine hours since he'd last heard her voice, and he craved the comfort that talking to her gave him.

Logan left a message, frowning as he hung up the phone. He wasn't going to be right again until she was here, safe and sound. Even now, he regretted leaving her to drive back on her own. But then, Sunny usually got her own way.

That was one thing he was going to have to get used to if Sunny was going to be a part of his life. But it wasn't the worst thing in the world—to spend the rest of his life making her happy.

IT FELT GOOD TO BE BACK in her own bed. Sunny rolled over on her stomach and looked at the clock. She'd arrived back at Willimston a few days before and had planned to stay just a night before driving the extra day to Logan's ranch. But he'd insisted that he didn't need the campervan or trailer immediately and urged her to relax and enjoy some time at home.

Sunny sighed. It was nearly eight, at least four hours earlier than she'd been accustomed to rising at home. But her time on the road with Logan had changed a lot of her bad habits. And since Tally had arrived on the farm the day before yesterday, she'd been out of bed at first light, anxious to get the filly settled in her new surroundings.

Reaching over, she smoothed her hand along the empty side of the bed. There wasn't a moment during the day when she didn't miss having Logan near her. They talked a lot on the phone, but it wasn't the same. And though they missed each other, he'd been reluctant to set a time when they could get together again.

Sunny wasn't sure what had happened since they parted, but she suspected it had to do with his hasty departure from Perth. All he would say was that he was working on some serious business matters and that he'd tell her all about it when he saw her next. The problem was, Sunny didn't know when that would happen.

For now, she'd wait. She was learning to be patient, and Logan was a man who was worth waiting for. Even with a day's distance between them, she was certain of the depth of her feelings. They'd be together soon and there would be time to talk about all the challenges they were both facing and the future they'd have together.

Still, the physical distance did take its toll. It was impossible not to miss the intimacy they'd shared. The hours before she fell asleep were filled with thoughts of the pleasure they'd given each other in bed and out. They had barely scratched the surface of their desire and now they had to put it on hold.

She crawled out of bed. So she'd do what she'd been doing since she got home. She'd put on her riding clothes and spend the day in the paddock working with Padma and training Tally. After that, she'd groom them both and muck out their stalls and then, hopefully, she'd fall into bed that evening, completely exhausted.

Sunny got dressed in her breeches and boots, then pulled on a freshly washed shirt. Her helmet was sitting on the chair near the window where she'd tossed it the previous afternoon. She put it on her head and jogged down the stairs.

"Coffee, please," she said to Lily as she passed through the kitchen.

The housekeeper poured her a mug, and Sunny grabbed it, along with a croissant, as she passed by. "Thank you, Lily," she said with a smile. "You always take such good care of me."

As she walked back to the stables, she noticed an old campervan parked next to Logan's camper. She stopped and looked it over, her mind flashing back to that day she first met Logan. That day had completely changed her life. She couldn't help but wonder what the driver of this vehicle was doing at the farm.

As she rounded the corner of the stable and walked toward the paddock, she pulled on her gloves. Now that she'd bought Tally, she was anxious to find out how quickly the horse could learn. Though Padma had already been trained to jump when she arrived at the farm, it would be a challenge for Sunny to train a horse herself. The bond between them was already becoming strong and, hopefully, it would take them both to an Olympic championship in four years.

Sunny stopped short when she saw a girl standing on the gate, petting Tally's nose. She looked to be about ten or eleven years old, her skinny legs revealed by baggy shorts and her pale blond hair swept up in a ponytail.

"She likes Anzac biscuits," Sunny called out.

The little girl turned around, then quickly jumped off the fence, shoving her hands in her pockets as if she'd been caught doing something wrong.

"Sorry," she mumbled, her face turning scarlet. "My dad said I wasn't supposed to get out of the campervan."

"Oh, you don't have to be sorry."

"I just really wanted to see the horses. I love horses."

"Tally can be a pest when it comes to getting her biscuits. Go ahead, you can pet her." Sunny joined the girl at the gate. "What's your name?"

"Anna. Anna Fleming."

Sunny held out her hand. "I'm Sunny Grant."

The girl shook her hand, staring up at Sunny with wide eyes. "My dad said you lived here. I saw you on television. At the Olympics. We watched at the pub."

"Oh, dear," Sunny replied. "I was not very good, was I?"

"Your horse was pretty," she said.

"Do you ride?"

The girl shook her head. "I don't have a horse. We don't have a place. My dad and I, we live in our campervan."

Sunny tried to hide her surprise. "Your mom, too?"

Anna shook her head. "My mom left when I was three. It's just me and my dad."

Sunny smiled. "I lived in a campervan for a while, too. I really liked it. It was very cozy."

Her shoulders rose and fell in a weak shrug. "I'd like to live in a house. And maybe have a puppy. And sleep in a real bed."

"Maybe you will someday." Sunny paused. "Why have you come to the farm?"

"My dad is looking for work. He's really good with horses. He's worked on horse farms all over Australia."

Sunny drew a deep breath. "I'm going to go get some biscuits for Tally. Why don't you stay here and I'll be right back?"

She left Anna standing at the gate and headed to the stable office in search of Ed. She found him there, deep in conversation with a wiry man who looked a few years older than Logan. Sunny poked her head in the door. "Ed, I need to speak with you. Can you spare just a few seconds?"

"I'm in the middle of something," he said.

"This won't wait." She stood outside, and when he joined her, Sunny grabbed Ed's arm and pulled him along to the far end of the stable. "I want you to hire that guy. Fleming. I want you to hire him."

"Now, Sunny, I don't mind you getting yourself involved in the occasional purchase of a horse, but the hiring and firing of the stable staff on this farm is up to me. I make those decisions."

"I don't care. I want you to hire him."

"You don't even know him," Ed pointed out.

"He has a daughter, about ten years old. They're living out of that campervan. She's got no mother. And I think it might be important that she has a real home for a while. I think that home should be here." Sunny stared up into his eyes. "Please?"

He studied her for a long moment, then nodded. "All right," Ed muttered.

"Really?" Sunny asked. She threw her arms around him and gave him a fierce hug. "You're a nice guy, Ed."

"Hell, I was planning on hiring him anyway. He's got great experience, comes with fine references and knows as much about horses as I do."

Sunny stepped back. "Can we give him the house near the grove? It needs to be fixed up, but Lily and I could do that. It would be perfect for them. The girl could have her own bedroom, and it has a nice little garden."

"Fine with me. Now can I get back to my interview?"

"No worries," she said with a wide grin.

He strode back inside the stable, then stopped and turned to her. "Since when do you care about strange kids?"

"She needs a home, Ed. We've got something to offer her. And she wants to learn how to ride. I figure, I can help her with that."

"*You?* Teach a kid how to ride?" He chuckled softly and shook his head. "Now, there's something I never expected to hear." He ran his hand through his hair. "Miss Grant, I do believe that you grew up when I wasn't looking."

"It's about time, no?" she said with a grin. "I'm twenty-six years old."

"Yeah," he said. "It is about time." Ed paused. "Does this have anything to do with the trip you and Logan took?"

"It might," she said. "I'm not sure yet." Sunny gave him a wave. "Offer him a decent salary. He might be raising a budding equestrian."

Ed chuckled. "All right. But next time you see the Sunny Grant I used to know, tell her I like the new Sunny Grant a lot better."

"I'll do that. But I'm pretty sure we won't be seeing her around this place anymore."

Sunny found Anna waiting where she'd left her.

The girl turned and hopped off the gate as soon as she noticed her approach. "Did you get the biscuits?"

Sunny groaned. "I forgot. But that can wait. You're going to come with me and we're going to find you a proper riding habit."

Her eyes went wide. "But—I don't think my— Why?"

"Because you're going to be staying at the farm for a while. Ed is going to give your daddy a job. And if you're going to live here you're going to need to learn to ride. And I just happen to be a very, very good teacher—I think."

"You think?"

"I've never taught anyone before, but I think I'll be grand. What do you think?"

A wide smile broke across her serious expression. "You will be grand," Anna said, nodding.

Sunny slipped her arm around the girl's shoulders. "I think I have some old breeches in my closet. And I know I have a pair of boots that will fit you."

They started off toward the house and, as they walked, Sunny couldn't help but smile. Maybe Logan had changed her for good. Maybe he'd taught her to see people for what they were, to know them for the lives they led and not for what she saw on the surface.

She couldn't help but think about the child he'd been and the troubles he'd seen. If she could spare another child from that kind of insecurity, then she would. Anna Fleming would get a home for as long as she wanted one.

And maybe Sunny would get something, too. She had always thought that teaching children how to ride was something she might be good at. Riding had given her an incredible sense of power and purpose in her own crazy childhood. Perhaps, it might do the same for someone like Anna.

Sunny drew a deep breath and smiled. So many things had changed for her in the past few weeks. She sometimes didn't even recognize herself anymore. And maybe that was a good thing. The Sunny Grant that she once knew wasn't worthy of a man like Logan Quinn.

Now maybe she was.

IT HAD BEEN NEARLY four weeks since he'd last seen Sunny, and Logan was just a little more than nervous. There had been so many things that required his attention at the ranch that a day's drive into Brisbane had been an impossibility. A half-million dollars had just dropped into his lap and that wasn't something he took lightly, never mind the other half million waiting for him in Ireland.

It still hadn't really sunk in. It was as if fate had stepped in to make all his dreams come true. Only, fate had come in the form of an elderly Irish novelist with money to spare. Though he hadn't scheduled his trip to Ireland, he was anxious to go. Logan needed to explain to his great-aunt how much her help had meant to him.

He'd kept his news a secret from Sunny, choosing to get all his plans in order before he told her. All she knew was that his parents were fine and he was working on some financial issues with the farm. He could hear the worry in her voice when they spoke on the phone. But she hadn't pressed him for details, and for that he was glad. No matter what happened, Sunny always seemed to know exactly what to say and how to act. But he also knew that she would be there for him, in the bad times and the good.

He'd planned their future in his head, working out all the little details. As a former investment banker he knew the risks of putting all his money into property. He'd decided to look for a small place, something within his conservative budget. After that, he'd invest the remainder of his inheritance for their future.

There had been so many things to consider. Was it better to spend money and fix up the ranch and then sell it? Or should he sell it as is, keeping the price low so that someone with limited resources might buy it? How much closer could he afford to be to Willimston without significantly reducing the amount of land he wanted? How far away should he stay just in case things didn't work out?

Everything had required careful consideration. Decisions were made after deliberate thought. But in the end, he had decided to look at a farm thirty kilometers west of Willimston, a beautiful place that had everything he'd ever need to raise his horses. And a place that Sunny might, one day, want to call home.

It was all falling into place. He'd get the farm. Then, he'd get the girl. And after that, they'd get the horse. He'd already set aside money to buy Tally back from the breeder in Perth and, though he wasn't even sure they were interested in selling, for the first time in his life, he had the power and the money to make it happen.

Logan frowned. "One step at a time," he murmured. *First the farm, then the girl, then the horse.* He clutched the steering wheel of the new pickup. Impatience would be the end of him.

He'd always been cool under pressure, but the stakes had never been so high. His future happiness was at risk. But they'd never really talked about a commitment. They'd discussed holidays together a few times a year. They'd discussed the option of being "friends with benefits." They'd even discussed, for a short time, Sunny living with him instead of returning to her home and family. Never once had they come close to mentioning the C word—commitment.

And now, he was prepared to ask her for that. He was ready to move his entire life to be closer to her. Though he wanted to believe Sunny would say yes to his proposal, he couldn't be sure. Hell, he hadn't even decided what his proposal was.

The options ranged from dating to marriage and everything in between. Should they spend more time together, getting to know each other better? Or should he just jump in and risk it all with a proposal of marriage? Maybe they ought to live together first and make the serious decisions later.

He groaned softly. There was always the chance that she'd say no to everything. That their time apart had weakened the bond they shared. A curse slipped from his lips. Maybe he should have gotten the horse first and then gone after the girl. At least with Tally, he'd have something significant to offer her besides promises and an engagement ring.

The sign for Willimston Farm appeared, and Logan turned into the driveway, taking the same route he had on the very day he'd first met Sunny. All that seemed so long ago, though it was barely six weeks. So much had changed in that time that it was hard to remember his life without her.

He pulled the truck to a stop in front of the house, a nervous knot growing in his stomach. Grabbing the bouquet of flowers he'd picked up in town, Logan drew a deep breath. He jumped out of the truck and smoothed his hand over his shirt. Eight hours on the road had left him a little rumpled, but dressed in khakis and a pale blue shirt, he wanted to impress. He'd even managed a haircut before leaving. Raking his fingers through his hair, Logan stood at the front door of the house and pushed the button for the doorbell.

A few moments later, the door swung open. He expected to see Sunny, but instead, he saw an older woman. "I—I'm here for Sunny?"

She smiled. "Well, there you are," she said. "I'm Lily, the housekeeper. Sunny's back in the stables. She said you're to go on back and meet her there. I believe you know the way?"

Logan nodded and started down the steps. But then he turned back to Lily. "Do I look all right?"

"Oh, you look grand," she said with a warm smile.

"And the flowers?"

"Sunny loves flowers. Daisies are her favorite, but I expect you know that."

"No," he said. "I didn't. It was just a lucky guess. But it is good to know. I need to know things like that."

In truth, there were still huge gaps in what they knew of each other's lives. They'd talked about many subjects on their way to Perth, but some things, like her favorite flowers, had gone untouched. But that was what the future was for. There would be fun in the discovery.

As he approached the stables, he heard a shout from the paddock nearby. Logan strode around the corner of the building and looked over the fence to find Sunny sprawled in the soft dirt next to a rail jump. With a quiet curse, he hopped over the gate and ran to her.

"Are you all right?"

"I'm fine," she said breathlessly. "She just refused. She doesn't like the white rails."

Sunny sat up, wincing, then looked into his eyes. Her expression brightened and she laughed, throwing her arms around his neck. "You're here," she exclaimed. "And you brought me flowers."

Logan chuckled, reaching out to straighten her riding helmet. "I am. It took me a while." He handed her the bouquet.

"It took you too long." Sunny hugged him again and pulled him down into the dirt with her, rolling on top of him as they kissed.

At that moment, Logan didn't care about his new shirt or his clean khakis. He just wanted to lose himself in the taste of her mouth and the feel of her body. This is exactly what he'd needed all these weeks, the perfect antidote for his loneliness. His fingers tangled in her hair as he molded his mouth to hers.

He pulled her beneath him, his body already responding to the kiss in ways he couldn't control. But as he looked down into her beautiful face, he felt a nudge on his shoulder. Logan glanced back to find a horse—

With a soft curse, Logan scrambled to his feet. Startled by his sudden movement, Tally shied away, but Logan held out his hand to calm her. Sunny stood up and wrapped her arm around his waist. "Look who's here," she said.

"Jaysus, Sunny, what did you do?" He looked over at her. "Please tell me you didn't steal her."

"Of course not," she said, giggling at the thought. "I bought her. She's mine. Actually, she's yours if you want her. We can work out a nice deal. Or we could share her. I'm teaching Tally to jump. She'd been doing well until she refused this fence. I think she wanted to toss me into the dirt."

He stared at the horse, unable to believe what he was seeing. A lump of emotion blocked his ability to speak, and he pulled Sunny into his arms and pressed a kiss to the top of her head. "I can't believe you did this. Thank you."

"I couldn't let her go," Sunny said. She smoothed her hand over his cheek. "The same way I could never let you go. I love Tally as much as you do, Logan. And I love you even more." She turned her face up to his. "You're part of my life now. Not just for today or for tomorrow, but forever. And it wouldn't have been complete without the horse that brought us together."

Logan closed his eyes and hugged her tight. "I've been thinking the same thing, Sunny. We belong together. All three of us."

She kissed him, her lips soft and sweet against his. "You changed me, Logan," she murmured. "You made me want more for myself. And you made me want you. I can't be happy without you."

"I love you, too," he murmured, drawing her into another kiss, this one deep and delicious. When he finally pulled back, there were tears glittering in her eyes. "Are you going to tell me how you managed this?"

"I made him an offer he couldn't refuse," Sunny teased.

"And you drove her back yourself?"

Sunny sucked in a sharp breath. "Actually, no. I drove back, Tally flew. I didn't want to risk her safety. And she's a lot to take care of on the road. Tally arrived here the day before I got back, and she's been settling in just fine."

"You're an amazing woman," he murmured, bending close.

"Yes, I am. Are you only noticing that now?"

"No. I've known that all along."

His kissed her again and, suddenly, he couldn't seem to get enough of her. She was intoxicating, the scent of her hair, the taste of her lips, the feel of her curves. He ached to touch her the way he used to, skin to skin, his fingers exploring her naked body.

"Maybe we should find someplace private," she murmured. "You could take off your pretty new clothes. I don't want you to get them any dirtier."

"That sounds like a wonderful idea. But there's something else we need to discuss first."

"There's something more important than getting naked and making love to me?"

"Well, yes. For the moment, there is." He grabbed her hand then pulled her along toward the gate. "We're going for a drive. It's not far, but I really need to get your opinion."

"A drive? Now?"

Logan nodded. "I promise, it's about twenty minutes west of here."

"But I have to take care of Tally. She's still got her bridle and saddle on."

She turned to hurry back to the horse, but Logan scooped her up in his arms and tossed her over his shoulder. "That can wait."

"No!"

As they passed the stable, Ed walked out, a bemused expression on his face. "Well, I can see where this is going already. Do you need any help?"

Sunny pushed up and reached out her hand. "Can you—"

"I was talking to Logan," Ed said.

"Yeah, take care of Tally, will you? Sunny and I have some important business to take care of."

He didn't set her down until they reached the side of a shiny new red pickup truck. He opened the passenger side door. "Get in."

"This is yours?"

"Like it?"

"It's very…very new," she said, frowning.

Logan opened the door and she got inside. When he slipped in behind the wheel she was staring at him. "When did you get this truck? And where are we going?"

"I'll explain when we get there," he said.

"And where is there?"

"A real pretty horse farm about twenty minutes west of here. I'm thinking about buying it—if you like it."

Sunny reached out and grabbed the truck keys from his hand. "Wait a second. Where is all this money coming from? You bought a new truck and, now, you're buying a new farm? Is there something you're not telling me?"

"Did I tell you that I loved you?"

Sunny nodded.

"And did I tell you that someday, I'm going to marry you?"

Her jaw dropped and she blinked. "No."

"I'm getting ahead of myself. We'll talk about that later. Can I have my keys now?" She held them away from him and Logan leaned close and captured her lips in a very persuasive kiss.

"No! Did you just propose marriage to me?"

Logan reached into his pants pocket and pulled out the small velvet box, holding it out. "The keys for the box," he teased. "I know that I can't give you everything, Sunny. But I can give you myself, my heart and soul. My life. And my promise that I'll do my best to make you happy forever."

He opened the box and removed the simple diamond ring. "This doesn't have to mean we're getting married tomorrow. Or even next month or next year. But I want to spend the rest of my life with you, Sunny. And I want that life to start now. Is that something you would want, too?"

The next few seconds seemed like an eternity. Sunny stared at the ring then glanced up into Logan's eyes. A tear trickled from the corner of her eye and she brushed it away. "Yes," she finally said. "Yes, it's something I want. I think I've wanted it since the moment I met you."

He slipped the ring on her finger and found it a little too large. "That's one more thing I need to learn about you. Your ring size."

She stared down at her hand. "It doesn't matter. It's perfect just the way it is."

He leaned forward and pressed his forehead to hers. "I guess it's you and me now," he whispered.

She kissed him softly. "I guess it is. I wouldn't want it any other way." Sunny looked down at the ring again. "So you bought a new truck and you bought me a diamond ring. And you're buying a new farm. How many horses did you have to sell?"

"Not one," Logan said.

"But—"

He caught her lips in a kiss, his tongue tracing

the crease until she opened for him. "It's a really interesting story. Oh, and there's one more surprise."

"Another surprise? I'm not sure I can take any more surprises."

"You and I have to go to Ireland next month."

Sunny sat back in her seat. "All right, start the truck. You can explain the whole story to me on the way to your new place."

"*Our* new place," he corrected. Logan grinned. "It's a really, really good story. You're going to like it."

"I already do," she said with a smile that said so much more. "I already do."

Epilogue

"MISS QUINN?"

Aileen Quinn looked up from her computer, her reading glasses perched on the end of her nose. She took off the glasses and laid them on the desk, then motioned Ian Stephens in. It had been weeks since she'd first sent him to search for her family and, though he'd sent her progress reports, she knew he was coming to report on some important news.

"Sit, sit," she said, motioning to a chair. "So, you have found my great-nephew."

"I have. And he's been given a share of his inheritance as you instructed. I understand he's very anxious to meet you. He's asked that we arrange a visit at your earliest convenience."

Ian handed her a folder and she opened it to find photographs inside. She picked one up of a handsome young man with dark hair and a sweet smile. "This is him?"

"That is," he said. "His name is Logan Quinn. Your brother Tomas married late in life. He was nearly fifty and his bride was thirty. They had just one son, Daniel, who also married. He had two sons. Only one is still living and that's Logan. He runs a horse ranch in Queensland."

"What of Tomas?"

"He passed away in 1973 and his wife a few years later. He made some rather bad investments and the family lived a penniless existence for the most part. Tomas's son, Daniel, seems to have followed in his father's footsteps when it came to financial matters."

"You found him? He would know about his father. He'd be able to tell me about my brother."

"Unfortunately, the son, Logan, isn't sure where his father is right now. According to my man, Winthrop, Daniel moves around from job to job, mostly working at cattle and sheep stations in remote areas of the country. But Logan expects that his parents will be in contact at some point in the future."

"And tell me. How is this horse ranch doing?"

Ian forced a smile. "It's a rather rough affair as you can see from the next photo," he said. "I suspect Logan Quinn has been living on a shoestring and that the shoestring was been very badly frayed. I believe that the inheritance may have saved him from ruin."

"Good," Aileen said. "I've spent my life collecting wealth and now it's time I start giving it away. Who better than my family? Tell me more."

Ian smiled. "Of course, he's very anxious to meet you," he said. "I hope I haven't overstepped, but he's going to be arriving week after next."

She smiled and pressed her hand to her heart. "It's so soon. I'm not sure I—"

"I could always ring him and have him delay his trip, Miss Quinn. I just thought since he was anxious to meet you that—"

"No, no," she said, waving her hand. "It's just… well, I've lived my whole life thinking I was all alone in the world. And now, I have family. I have a great-nephew and he wants to meet me. I'm afraid we shouldn't delay."

"He's a very nice young man according to the report. Very grateful."

Aileen slowly stood. "I'd like you to continue to search for his parents. And what news have you regarding my other siblings?"

"Good news on your brother Diarmuid. We've tracked him to the States. He found a job on a passenger liner when he was sixteen and worked until he could buy his own passage. He landed in New York City in 1923, but we haven't been able to trace him further. There are some very hopeful leads, though, and I'm certain we're going to have a breakthrough very soon."

Aileen circled the huge mahogany desk and sat down on the chair next to Ian. "You've done wonderful work, Mr. Stephens, and in such a short time.

But I'm sure you'll understand when I tell you that you must work even faster."

"Yes, ma'am, I understand. I will hire more investigators. And I'm certain that I'll have much more at our next meeting."

She reached out and took his hand, patting it as she spoke. "I'm sure you'll understand why time is of the essence. I've lived without a family all these years. I'd like to know them before I leave this mortal coil."

As she walked him to the door, Aileen slipped her hands around his arm. Their footsteps were soft on the old Chinese carpet. She walked outside and waved goodbye as he drove off in his little sports car.

There was nothing like family, she thought to herself. And now, she'd meet this young man, this Logan Quinn. Would she recognize something of herself in him? In the way he spoke or the way he laughed? Or was their connection so distant that there would be nothing that bound them together except blood?

"A horse rancher," she said to herself. "My, he sounds like he'd be an interesting young man." She hurried back into the house. "Sally? Sally?"

The housekeeper came running out into the entry hall, her hand pressed to her chest. "Yes. Yes, I'm here. What is it? Oh, sweet Jesus, I thought you'd fallen. You sounded so panicked."

"Just excited," Aileen said. "We're going to have a houseguest in a few weeks. My great-nephew will be visiting from Australia. I think we need to freshen up the guest rooms. Maybe do a bit of redecorating. I want to make sure my family feels comfortable here."

"Yes, ma'am. Why don't the two of us sit down and have some lunch and we'll go over all the details?"

"Details," she said. "I have so many details. Mr. Stephens put them all in his report. Did I tell you his name was Logan? That sounds like such a lovely name. I wonder what he likes to eat?"

"I don't know. Maybe we should start planning some menus."

Aileen took the housekeeper's arm as they slowly walked back inside the house. "Family is a wonderful thing, isn't it?"

* * * * *

COMING NEXT MONTH FROM

Available February 19, 2013

#739 A SEAL'S SURRENDER • *Uniformly Hot!*
by Tawny Weber

Cade Sullivan always knew he was meant to be a SEAL. Heck, he'd been pulling cute little Eden Gillespie out of scrapes from the time they were kids. But now Cade is home and Eden has turned into a *very* sexy woman. So who's going to save her this time—from him?

#740 MAKING HIM SWEAT
by Meg Maguire

When matchmaker Jenna Wilinski learns she's inherited a shady Boston boxing gym, she's not sure what to do. Suddenly, she's surrounded by men—hot and sweaty ones! But once she meets Mercer Rowley, she's tempted to work up a sweat herself....

#741 SIZZLE
by Kathy Garbera

Remy Stephens can whip up a feast of sensual delights, but so can Staci Rowland. These two reality show contestants are battling it out for the title of Premier Chef. But are they cooking up a storm in the kitchen—or in the bedroom?

#742 SMOOTH SAILING • *Stop the Wedding!*
by Lori Wilde

To convince his ex to give him another chance, reformed billionaire bad boy Jeb Whitcomb sets sail for Key West, only to fall for his accidental stowaway Haley French—the one woman he's never impressed, until now....

YOU CAN FIND MORE INFORMATION ON UPCOMING HARLEQUIN® TITLES, FREE EXCERPTS AND MORE AT WWW.HARLEQUIN.COM.

HBCNM0213

REQUEST YOUR FREE BOOKS!
2 FREE NOVELS PLUS 2 FREE GIFTS!

red-hot reads!

When matchmaker Jenna Wilinski learns
she's inherited a shady Boston boxing gym,
she's not sure what to do. But once she meets
Mercer Rowley, she's tempted to work up a
sweat herself....

Here's a sneak peek at

Making Him Sweat

by rising star, Meg Maguire

Jenna swallowed, her gaze dropping to Mercer's chest before
she caught herself and hoisted it back up to his face. Shutting
the cabinet, she mustered the nerve to ask, "How would you
feel if I moved in before you moved out?"

"So, we'd be roommates until I find my next place?" When
she nodded, he shrugged. "I guess I can put up with anybody
for two weeks."

She looked down to hide her grin. She could sense him
smiling back, could feel his closeness as tangibly as sunshine
warming her skin. Dangerous.

"And hell," he said, leaning an arm along the door frame
and bringing his face a little closer to hers, something hot and
unwelcome spiking Jenna's pulse. Mercer smirked. "Maybe us
shacking up together is just the chance I need to grow on
you—change your mind about ruining all our lives."

Praying he couldn't see how his nearness had flushed her

cheeks, she ignored his challenge. "It'll save me a chunk of change on a hotel."

"You're the boss."

The boss. An intriguing notion. Boss to a small, inherited army of brutes for now. To a well-groomed team of assistants in a few weeks' time, all things going as planned.

In the sunlight, his hazel eyes were the warm, brownish-green of a ripe pear. His gaze was direct, intense as a flood-light. It seemed as though he was reading her thoughts. For a long moment, they just stared at one another. Too long a moment.

She swallowed, her gaze flitting from his bare arm to the shape of his chest, the stubble peppering his jaw and the curve of his lower lip. He mirrored the scrutiny, an expression of curiosity in his gaze.

"I've got an extra set of keys down in the office, if you want them today." His voice sounded so *close*.

"That'd be good." She inwardly sighed, feeling too many things. Overwhelmed, elated, terrified. *Attracted*. "Thank you," she said. "I know it's probably not easy being this courteous to me…."

"What choice have I got?"

"Because I'm your boss?"

"Nah. Because I loved your dad. And he loved you. So I have to at least pretend to respect your wishes." He grinned. "Although they really suck…."

Pick up MAKING HIM SWEAT by Meg Maguire, available February 19.

It's getting hot in here!

Remy "Stephens" is hot in the kitchen and, as Staci Rowland discovers, out of it, as well. These two battle it out for the title of Premier Chef, cooking up a storm in the kitchen *and in the bedroom!*

Pick up

Sizzle

by *Katherine Garbera*

AVAILABLE FEBRUARY 19, 2013

HARLEQUIN®

Blaze®

Red-Hot Reads

www.Harlequin.com

HB79745

HARLEQUIN®

A *Romance* FOR EVERY MOOD™

Stay up-to-date on all your
romance-reading news with the
Harlequin Shopping Guide,
featuring bestselling authors, exciting new
miniseries, books to watch and more!

The newest issue will be delivered right to you
with our compliments! There are 4 each year.

Signing up is easy.

EMAIL

ShoppingGuide@Harlequin.ca

WRITE TO US

HARLEQUIN BOOKS
Attention: Customer Service Department
P.O. Box 9057, Buffalo, NY 14269-9057

OR PHONE

1-800-873-8635 in the United States
1-888-343-9777 in Canada

Please allow 4-6 weeks for delivery of the first issue by mail.

Love the Harlequin book you just read?

Your opinion matters.

Review this book on your favorite book site, review site, blog or your own social media properties and share your opinion with other readers!